THE RED BLAZER GIRLS

for Laura

THE RED BLAZER GIRLS

The Ring of Rocamadour

MICHAEL D. BEIL

SCHOLASTIC INC.
New York Toronto London Auckland
Sydney Mexico City New Delhi Hong Kong

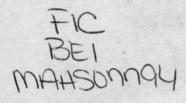

FIC
BEI
MAHSOnngy

This is a work of fiction. Names, characters, places, and incidents are the product of the author's imagination or are used fictitiously. Any resemblance to actual persons, living or dead, events, or locales is entirely coincidental.

No part of this publication may be reproduced, stored in a retrieval system, or transmitted in any form or by any means, electronic, mechanical, photocopying, recording, or otherwise, without written permission of the publisher. For information regarding permission, write to Yearling, an imprint of Random House Children's Books, a division of Random House, Inc., 1745 Broadway, New York, NY 10019.

ISBN 978-0-545-27656-6

12 11 10 9 8 7 6 5 4 3 2 1   10 11 12 13 14 15/0

Printed in the U.S.A.   40

First Scholastic printing, September 2010

The text of this book is set in Bookman.

Chapter 1

In which I enter an alternative universe where burly men read Cosmo and giant house cats roam sacred corridors

For as far back as I can remember, I have told everyone I know that I am going to be a writer. And it's not just some idle dream. I have been a busy girl, and my hard drive is bulging with the results of this ambition: a heaping assortment of almost-but-not-quite-finished short stories and at least three this-time-I'm-really-off-to-a-great-start-and-I-mean-it novels. Unfortunately, every single thing I have written—until now, that is—is fatally flawed. "Write what you know!" everyone told stubborn little me. Very good advice—that I completely ignored. Instead, I wrote and wrote, filling my stories to the brim with people and places I have spent my life *reading* about instead of the people and places that *are* my life. But all that changed the moment I looked out the window in Mr. Eliot's English class and screamed. Suddenly I had my very own story.

My tale begins in September, my first month in the "upper school" at St. Veronica's, on the Upper East Side of Manhattan. I know, I know—it sounds snobby, like one of those schools in the movies or TV, but trust me, it's not. Believe me, I'm not rich, and my friends aren't either. St. V's is just a nice, ordinary all-girls' school that just happens to be in a pretty expensive neighborhood. Yes, we wear plaid skirts with our lovely red blazers, and yes, there are a few nuns running around the place, but there are no limos parked outside or helicopters on the roof or anything like that.

We are just starting *Great Expectations* in Mr. Eliot's English class, taking turns reading aloud from the first chapter. So Leigh Ann Jaimes is reading. Someday, Leigh Ann, a very passionate reader, *will* win an Academy Award. When she reads, it's like one of those fabulous, a-star-is-born auditions for a Broadway play. *Great Expectations,* the "greatest novel ever written" per our Mr. Eliot, starts off with this spooky scene: as a cold early-evening fog hangs over a churchyard cemetery, the poor little orphan Pip is wandering near his parents' headstone. As Leigh Ann pours her heart into every word, I'm picturing the mist hanging over the graves, worn smooth by the passage of time. I feel the chilly, clammy air, hear the trees creaking and swaying in the wind, and so there I am, perched on the edge of my seat, when Leigh Ann reads: *"'Hold your noise!' cried a terrible voice, as a man started up from among the graves at the side of the church porch. 'Keep still, you little devil, or I'll cut your throat!'"*

I gasp. Loudly.

Leigh Ann, along with everyone else in the room, spins around to look at me.

"Everything all right, Miss St. Pierre?" Mr. Eliot asks, peering over his glasses and trying to hold back a smile. Mr. Eliot is one of those teachers who is basically cool, but still a total geek—always making really corny jokes that only he gets. His first name is George, which explains a lot. Get it? George Eliot, like the novelist? Except that *that* George Eliot was really a woman named Mary Ann Evans. Oy.

I blush—just a little. "I'm fine. Thanks for asking though." Always keep 'em guessing—that's what I say.

He nods to Leigh Ann to continue.

Across the room, my best friend Margaret Wrobel has this *huge* smile on her face. She mouths the words "deep breaths" at me, which is what she always tells me when I get too excited, or too scared, or too anxious, or too anything. I'm a very emotional person—I just don't seem to have that "whatever" gene. *Everything* matters in my world.

Margaret reads next, and her version of Charles Dickens is flavored with a soupçon of a Polish accent, a remnant of the first seven years of her life in the suburbs of Warsaw. My eyes drift off for a moment, turning to the stained glass windows and the gray stone walls of

St. Veronica's Church, separated from the school by a courtyard that is maybe twenty or thirty feet wide.

And then I scream. And this time, I am at least as startled as everyone else in the room, with the possible exception of poor Mr. Eliot.

"Sophie! For crying out *loud*. I know it's an exciting book, but *please* try to control yourself."

"I'm sorry, Mr. Eliot, but I saw—" I point out the window at the church, but the thing that had been so scream-worthy is gone.

"Yes?"

"Nothing. I thought I saw something, but it must have just been a pigeon."

"My gosh. What was this pigeon *doing*?"

The bell rings (yay!) and I gather my books quietly and glance furtively out the window, hoping to get a second look at what I had seen for just the briefest flash.

Margaret and I walk to the locker we share.

"So, what was *that* all about?" she demands, after we get away from the crowd outside the room.

"I saw something," I whisper.

"Something like . . . dead people?" Margaret whispers back.

Rebecca Chen sticks her head in between Margaret and me. "What's going on? Why are we whispering?"

"Sophie says she saw something scary out the window during English class. She actually screamed."

Rebecca's interest level increases immediately. "You *screamed*? In class? Cool."

4

"I saw a face in the window. That little round one in the church. C'mon, I'll show you."

We return to the now-empty Room 503 and re-create the scene.

"I was sitting right here, and for just a split second, I saw it, plain as day. A woman's face, really pale, almost white, with long white hair."

"You dozed off," says Rebecca. "It was a dream."

"No, I was wide awake. You know how sometimes you're sitting there with the remote, and you're flipping through the channels as fast as you can, but every once in a while you see something—something you recognize, like a cute guy, or a scene from your favorite episode of *Seinfeld* or whatever—and even though you only saw it for like a split second, you still take it in? Well, that's what it was like."

"Sophie, we're on the fifth floor," Margaret says. "That means we're forty feet up. That window is above us—it's probably just an attic or something. Sorry, but it's pretty unlikely that there was an old lady at that window."

"Unless it was a ghost!" Rebecca is getting more excited by the minute. "Or someone trapped! Or being held in a secret room, like in *The Man in the Iron Mask*!"

Margaret, the smartest person I know, can't resist an opportunity for a good literary allusion. "Or maybe she's in the church seeking sanctuary, like Quasimodo. You know, *The Hunchback of Notre Dame*."

A couple of years ago, Margaret's dad salvaged a complete set of the Harvard Classics that some moron

5

in their building had put out with the trash. Margaret has made it one of her missions in life to read all seventy volumes.

"Guys, I'm serious. I know you don't believe me, and I don't blame you, but I swear I saw her. And, uh, the weird part is, even though I only saw her for a second, I got the strangest feeling that she was trying to say something to me."

"Like what?" Rebecca asks, eyes wide.

"Like she needed help or something." I wait for them to scoff.

"Look, Soph, I know you well enough to know you wouldn't scream unless you saw *something*, so if you say you saw her, we believe you. Don't we, Rebecca?"

Rebecca looks dubious but goes along. "Ooookaaaayyy. I mean, yes. Absolutely. I believe you. Do you believe I'm starving? Can we go to lunch now?"

"C'mon, Bec. Lunch can wait. We have a mission. I have a granola bar in my bag—it's full of oaty, nutty goodness, and it's all yours."

"Really? You think we should go right now?" I can pass up lunch—especially a school lunch—for a little adventure.

"Why wait? If it is a ghost, this could be the one day in the year that she shows herself, you know, like the anniversary of the day she was murdered. We have to go *now*."

Rebecca positively lights up at the mention of

murder. "Okay, you guys, but I have to be back in time for English. I walked in ten seconds after the bell yesterday and Mr. Smelliot gave me the stink-eye. I don't think he likes me."

"We have lots of time," Margaret replies. "Thirty-five minutes. And Mr. Eliot likes everybody."

"Hand over the granola bar," Rebecca commands. "Sheesh, no wonder you're such a twig."

Margaret leads the way. Somehow she knows the back way into the church—through a door that I'd walked past a million times without ever bothering to wonder what was on the other side, and then up a narrow staircase illuminated by a single bare lightbulb. At the top of the stairs, she pushes open another door (which groans like a grumpy old man), and just like that, we are in the church foyer about six feet from the security guard.

He has a full head of white hair that stands straight up in that fifties style—cut perfectly flat on top. Makes me want to set a vase on it. He looks up from, oddly enough, the latest issue of *Cosmopolitan*.

Margaret steps right up to his desk. "Hi! We're students over at St. V's and we were just wondering if it would be all right if we took a look around the church. I mean, we come over here for Masses, but we never get to really see the church that much. Is that okay?"

He holds a hand up to his left ear, which is outfitted with a rather large hearing aid. "Say again. Didn't quite get you."

"IS IT OKAY IF WE TAKE A LOOK AROUND? WE'RE FROM THE SCHOOL." She points at the crest on her blazer.

He squints through his fingerprint-smudged, thick lenses. "School's around the corner." I note that he is taking the *Cosmo* quiz—"Pushy or Pushover?"

"Let me try." I move closer to the ear without the hearing aid. "Excuse me." No response. "EXCUSE ME!" He looks up and I hold out my camera. "WE JUST WANT TO LOOK AROUND. MAYBE TAKE SOME PICTURES. IS THAT OKAY?"

"No flash." And he turns the page to "If It's Not One Thing, It's Your Mother" (note to self: pick up this issue for future reference).

"Well, that was interesting," says Rebecca as we wander through the double doors and into the actual church.

"If we can't sneak by *him,* we are without a doubt the worst snoops in history," Margaret declares.

St. Veronica's is pretty spectacular, and I am actually looking forward to a little "snooping." But Margaret is all business.

"We have to figure out a way to get up there." She points to a series of arches at least thirty or forty feet above us on the wall of the opposite side of the church. "If you were looking from Mr. Eliot's room, that's about the right height."

"What's this part of the church called?" I ask.

"The long part, from the doors to the altar, where the highest part of the ceiling is, is called the nave. This part, where we are, that goes across the nave, is the transept." She emphasizes the "trans" so I am sure to get it. (Margaret is *very* big on vocabulary—root words and prefixes and all that stuff.) "If you were to look down on the church, it's shaped like a big cross."

"I never realized that. Makes sense, though. How do you know all this again?"

"Victor Hugo."

"Ahh. Thank God and the Harvard Classics."

"Amen," says Margaret. "Now, do you see where those confessionals are?" She points to the three identical wooden doors where parishioners go to confess their sins. (Now here's a confession for you: sometimes I "embellish" my own confessions to make them more penance-worthy. Pretty sad, huh? All in all, I'm a distressingly good girl.) "Now look to the right of them. See that door? *That's* where we need to go first."

We aren't too concerned with Robert, the security guard—and I use that title loosely—but we still try to look *très* nonchalant as we make our way to the door we have targeted. It is near a painting on the right side of the church, and we suddenly become *very* interested in all the artwork. The door is heavy, built of dark, deeply carved wood with a grid of twisted iron over a stained glass picture of a golden chalice.

"Zee Holy Grail. Very Monty Python." Rebecca,

assuming this really bad French accent, quotes one of her favorite lines: "I fart in your general direction."

We all giggle because, let's face it, saying the word "fart" in church is deeply wrong and funny.

I put my hand on the doorknob and look at Margaret. "What do you think?"

Margaret is nervous but determined. She knows her parents would kill her if she got into any trouble. She takes an audible deep breath: "Go ahead. Try it."

I try turning the knob. Locked. "Now what?"

"Let me see." Margaret kneels in front of the door. "This lock is ancient. Rebecca? Can you pick it?"

Rebecca joins Margaret on the floor, inspecting the lock. "Got a bobby pin?"

Suddenly Margaret stands up. "Someone's coming. Look interested in the painting."

A middle-aged man in a chocolate-brown suit several sizes too big appears from behind the altar, straightening candles and trimming wicks. Margaret coughs, and he looks up, a bit surprised to see us.

"Good afternoon, young ladies." He comes closer and looks up at the painting of the sixth Station of the Cross, *Veronica Wipes the Face of Jesus*. "Beautiful, isn't it? Captures the weightiness of Christ's burdens, don't you think? It's my favorite."

I have spent enough time with my parents in museums in New York and Paris to have at least a vague idea of great art, and this ain't it. Rebecca, the artistic one among us, could do much better. We all nod in agreement anyway.

"We're doing a class project. Do you happen to know who the artist was? It doesn't appear to be signed."

Oh, yeah, my friend Margaret, she's smooth.

"It's no one famous. Sadly, we can't display any truly valuable art anymore. We've had a few pieces by better-known artists stolen right off the walls. Can you imagine—stealing from a church! All fourteen Stations of the Cross were painted in the 1930s by a former parishioner, a Mr. Harriman. There are several more of his paintings in the rectory. Mostly copies of Caravaggio." (*Bad* copies, I'll bet!) "His granddaughter is still a parishioner; in fact, she lives right next door." He lifts the bottom corner of the painting and pulls it away from the wall, examining the back. "Ah, there it is. 'M. Harriman 1934.' " He then sticks out his hand to each of us and smiles pleasantly. "I'm Gordon Winterbottom, the church deacon."

I smile politely as I shake his hand with the firm grip my dad taught me to use. "Hi, I'm Sophie St. Pierre, and this is Margaret Wrobel and Rebecca Chen."

As he shakes Margaret's and Rebecca's hands, I get a better look at him. It isn't only his suit that seems not to fit, it's like his *skin* is two sizes too big, too. It hangs down in flaps around his cheeks and is the color of old cheese. But even though he absolutely reeks of cigarettes, he *seems* nice enough. Don't judge, I think to myself. My dad was an enthusiastic smoker until Mom became pregnant with me, and he's always telling Mom that her labor pains were nothing compared to what he went through while he was trying to kick the habit.

"Pleasure to meet you girls. Seventh grade?"

"Do we look *that* lost?" I say.

He laughs—sort of a half laugh, half lung-about-to-come-flying-out-his-throat cough. "No, it isn't that. Mostly it's the blazers. The high school girls' blazers start to look a little shopworn. Your lapels are still nice and crisp."

The guy is good. A week earlier, the entire seventh grade went through St. Veronica's elaborate "Blazer Day Ceremony," in which we traded in the red sweater vests of the lower school for the plaid skirts and shockingly red (*crimson*, officially) blazers of the upper school with the crest that reads *Maiestas et dignitas*. Very cool. Really.

"Our blazers *are* new," Margaret says. "My, you could be a detective."

"Maybe I have missed my true calling," he says with a jaunty wink. "Well, I'll leave you to your research. If you have any questions, don't be afraid to ask. Of course, I don't have *all* the answers—I'm just the deacon. But perhaps one of the priests can help."

Wait a second. Was that a note of sarcasm in his voice? Or just your basic New York attitude? I'm detecting a bit of a Brooklyn accent.

"Thank you," I say. "I think we have what we need."

"So far, at least," adds Margaret. He returns to the altar while Rebecca bends my bobby pin into a makeshift key, and ten seconds later, we hear a click.

Rebecca looks up, grinning. She turns the knob and pushes the door open a few inches, just enough to look inside. Then she gasps and pulls the door shut.

"Oh my God!"

"What is it? What's in there?"

"Gotcha!" she says, laughing at our shocked expressions.

Margaret shakes her head and nudges past Rebecca. "Hilarious. Let me see."

Rebecca checks the door to make sure it won't lock behind us and pushes it open the rest of the way. "After you, m'lady."

Margaret strides right in, with Rebecca and me hustling after her into the unknown. When Rebecca gently closes the door, all is suddenly quite dark. The sounds of Lexington Avenue penetrate the front portion of the church, but once we pass through that door, it is so quiet I can hear my heart whim-whamming. A cold draft comes right through the stone walls and shimmies out into the darkness. Rebecca elbows me, pointing out the image of the stained glass chalice at my feet, projected onto the floor by the dim light of the church.

I feel goose bumps popping up under my blazer. "This is more *Indiana Jones* than Monty Python," I whisper.

The church isn't that old—it was built around 1900—but I feel like I am back in the Middle Ages. The floor, the windowless walls, the arched ceiling, are all made of roughly cut stone; it seems more like a cave than a hallway. Last summer vacation, my parents took me into some catacombs beneath a church in Paris where there are *thousands* of people buried. Reeeaaaally creepy, and definitely *not* something I want to discover here in St. V's.

Margaret leads us deeper into the abyss. "There must be another passage directly above us."

"Or a crypt," says Rebecca, reinforcing my fear that we're about to stumble onto a bunch of final resting places.

And suddenly there it is—an incredibly dark, low-ceilinged, twisting, narrow, scary staircase.

"Do you think—" Rebecca starts, but by the time she gets to "think," Margaret's feet are the only part of her still in sight.

Up and up and round and round we go till we find ourselves standing at the end of another long passage-way, lighted—barely—by two porthole-size, grime-covered windows set into the two-foot-thick walls. I wipe away some of the schmutz from the one closest to me and take a peek outside. I am looking straight at my desk in Mr. Eliot's room! When I move to the other window, I see that it has recently been wiped clean.

"Regarde!" I say.

"Holy crap!" says Rebecca.

"Practically proof positive," says Margaret.

Then, from the end of the hall, a door hinge squeaks one short *errkkkk*. We stare at the shaft of light coming from inside the heavy wooden door as an enormous orange cat squeezes through the opening. Roughly the size of a small car, the cat takes a few steps down the hall before it sees us. Then it arches its back, every hair on its body standing straight up—kind of like the ones on the back of my neck are doing—and then makes a god-awful hissing, spitting, growling yowl.

"Go 'way, hellcat! Shoo. Shoo," says Rebecca, backing up. "I don't think it likes us." She turns and runs for the stairs.

Margaret and I are on her heels, but then I hear it—a woman's voice, with an accent that sounds a lot like Margaret's mom's. Polish? Russian?

I freeze. "Listen!" We all strain to hear the voice coming from behind that door.

". . . I don't know *where* she found it, but it's definitely something from *him*. She said something about a card or a letter, and needing to get into the school library. This could be what we've been waiting for, after all these years. And it's about time. I don't know how much more of that old dingbat I can take."

Margaret and I look at each other. The school library?

"Hold on a second," the voice continues, sounding harried. "She's looking for that damned cat. He must have gotten out again. I have to go—she's coming up the stairs." I hear her set the phone down. We are trapped between that open door, whoever—or whatever—is coming up the stairs, and the demon feline.

And that's when I hear the second voice, this one belonging to a much older woman.

"Can you help me catch my kitty? He likes to go down those old stairs."

I slowly turn to face the voice—is it an elderly female Quasimodo, freshly sharpened edge of her ax glistening inches above my head? Nah. Standing before me is a tiny old lady. She has long, straight hair that appears to be nearly pure white in that dark hallway, but her skin is remarkably smooth and unwrinkled, making it difficult to tell how old she is. Fifty? Seventy? Clothing-wise, she looks like some kind of sixties flower child—a floor-length, tie-dyed tunic with six or seven strands of different-colored beads paired with Birkenstocks. It is the woman from the window. No doubt about it.

I must have a frightened look on my face, because she smiles reassuringly at me. "It's all right, dear. I'm not going to hurt you. Even if I wanted to, I don't think I could."

Hellcat, halfway between us, roars as if to add, *"But I could."*

"Oh, don't worry about him," she says as I back away. "He's a darling old fuddy-duddy. All hiss and no bite. I must not have latched the door, and he just lets himself out. That *was* you I saw a little while ago, wasn't it? I'm sorry if I spooked you. But how nice of you to come looking for me."

"I wasn't scared," I lie. "Just a little . . . surprised."

"Well, Teazle just *knew* you were coming. He's been carrying on all morning. This is the second time I've found him out here in the hallway—why, we might never have met if not for him. You know, I've always suspected he's a bit psychic—perhaps the reincarnation of my dear old great-aunt Maysie. Now *she* was gifted. Predicted the stock market crash in twenty-nine. Her father never forgave her for not telling *him*."

Eyes wild, Margaret's face finally appears around the bend in the staircase, with Rebecca an inch behind.

"Well, hello to you all. I'm Elizabeth Harriman, and this big ol' monster is Teazle." She hoists him off the ground, holding him the way I used to hold my dolls, his feet hanging down almost to her knees. Still shaking a bit, and wary of the cat, I sort of grope her hand as we introduce ourselves.

"Won't you girls come in for a cup of tea?"

Come in *where*? Where did she come from?

Rebecca speaks up. "Um, Sophie, the bell's in like two minutes."

"Oh, dear," said Ms. Harriman. "Well, might you come back after school, mmm? I have something *very* important to ask you."

We all look at each other. "Are you guys in?" I ask.

"Uh, sure," says Rebecca.

"Absolutely," says Margaret.

Really? What are we getting ourselves into?

"Wonderful! Shall we say three o'clock?"

"Should we come back *here*?" I look uncertainly at the dimly lit passageway.

"Oh. No. Just come to my front door on Sixty-fifth Street. Right next door to the school. My home is the old convent, back when there were more nuns around. That's why it is connected to the church. It's the bright red door—just like your blazers. You've probably walked past it a thousand times. Ring the bell. Teazle and I will be waiting for you. Young ladies, I think karma has brought us to this fortuitous meeting. Our fates have become intertwined."

"Um, see you at three," I say, and we hustle the heck out of there.

Chapter 2

In which I share a chair with a dead guy and listen to an amazing story

The rest of that day flies by. What awaits us *inside* the home of Ms. Elizabeth Harriman? Rooms crammed full of lava lamps, beaded curtains, and paintings of Janis Joplin on black velvet? Jimi Hendrix music blasting on the hi-fi?

Precisely at three o'clock, I press the doorbell at the red door of her town house. I put my ear to the brass mail slot. The door opens suddenly, and I tumble face-first into the chest of a granite block of a woman. Her hair—or is it a helmet?—is the color of an overcast November day, and she's wearing a plain white apron with the name "Winnie" embroidered on her formidable bosom.

"Hello, misses. Ms. Harriman, she's waiting for you. Come in."

As she turns away, we shoot glances at one another. It was *her* voice we'd heard talking on the telephone earlier.

"Thank you, Winifred," says Ms. Harriman, who

immediately starts asking questions—and answering them almost as quickly. "Come in, girls, please. Make yourselves at home. Would you like something to drink? Winifred, bring us some tea, would you, dear? A big pot of Flower Power seems appropriate." Then, insisting that we call her Elizabeth and *not* Ms. Harriman (something I just can't bring myself to do), she leads us into the biggest living room I've ever seen, full of tasteful leather and dark wood furniture on Oriental rugs—not a bean bag chair or shag rug in sight.

Wandering around a bit, I start to get a sense of the sheer ginormosity of the place. I am in immediate awe of the staircase's curved, carved banister.

"Jeez, this place is *huge*. How many floors are there?" I ask.

"The house has five floors, but I rarely use the top three these days. My room is on the second floor, and Winifred uses the third for ironing and some other chores. The top floor, where Teazle snuck out the door earlier, is the old servants' quarters; it's badly in need of renovating, I'm afraid. The house has been in my family for three generations."

Man, to have a few extra *floors*. In my family's apartment, we'd all love to have an extra *drawer*.

These walls are covered with modern paintings— I recognize a Picasso, a Matisse, and two Warhols—and I'm pretty sure they are the real thing. Jeez, who *is* this lady?

"I see you're admiring the paintings," she says. "Are you an art lover, Sophie?"

"Me? Uh, yeah, I guess I am. But Rebecca's the real artist; you should see her sketchbook—"

"Sophie, please," Rebecca interrupts, and then blushes fourteen shades of pink—all the way to fuchsia.

"What? You're an amazing artist. Go on, show her your book. It's great."

Ms. Harriman comes to Rebecca's rescue. "I *would* love to see it sometime, Rebecca. Maybe after we get to know each other a little better, mmm?"

"Fine." Rebecca exhales and her face returns to a more natural color. "But I'm really not that great. Not compared to . . ." She waves her hand around the room.

"Pshaw," says Ms. Harriman. "All these artists started out just like you."

This makes my friend smile. I don't think she's ever thought of famous artists in that way.

Winifred, who has been hovering nearby, serves tea with a plate of unmemorable cookies (being the daughter of a French chef, I am a bit of a cookie snob) and Ms. Harriman starts to ask all about us—our families, how we do in school, what we do for fun, the whole enchilada. She is fascinated by Margaret's stories of growing up in Poland and how her family picked up their lives and moved to New York. Then it's Rebecca's turn. Ms. Harriman's eyes water as Rebecca tells her about her dad dying when she was seven, leaving her mom with three little kids. I am a little surprised, because it is something Rebecca *never* talks about. My own story isn't as interesting, but I tell her all about my dad, who grew up in France and is now the sous chef at a très chic restaurant in Midtown (a place that seems a bit obsessed with goose livers, if you ask me), and my mom—a "real" New Yorker, born and raised in Queens—who teaches violin at a very famous music school on the West Side and also plays in a string quartet that has performed at Carnegie Hall and recorded two CDs.

And right when I'm beginning to think that she's just a lonely old lady looking for someone to talk to, she says, "So, I suppose you're wondering if I'm ever going to tell you why I asked you to come. You've been very patient, and I appreciate your indulging an old woman." She takes a deep breath, sits back in her chair, and tells us her story.

"To begin, my father, Everett Harriman, was a well-known archaeologist. He taught at Columbia for over forty years and traveled all over the world, especially to Europe and the Middle East. Even though I was not trained or formally educated as an archaeologist, he took me along on many of his expeditions because he trusted me—and I was the only one who could decipher his notes from the field. We had a wonderful relationship. The time we spent in dusty old tents, reading poetry and talking about art, and literature, and politics—those were the happiest days of my life. Father was one of the leading authorities on Christianity during the second and third centuries, and wrote several books on the subject. The Metropolitan Museum has many of the pieces that he collected."

She stops while Winnie refills our cups with the oddly appealing Flower Power tea, and then she carries on.

"With all the travel and the fieldwork and the research and writing, the years seemed to fly past. Before I knew it, I was thirty and unmarried, but I didn't mind—I had a great life. And then I met Malcolm. Malcolm Chance. He was a young colleague of Father's at Columbia, one of the 'new breed' of archaeologists. A little too sloppy with his research, a little lazy. More interested in fame and glory than meticulous scholarship. I didn't care—he was gorgeous. You girls know the type: tall, dark, handsome—like someone out of a romance novel. We were married, and a few years later, I had a beautiful little girl, my Caroline. You girls remind me so much of her—so bright, so full of life. Caroline read everything she could get her hands on. She could have gone to any school in the city, but she wanted to be close to home, so we chose St. Veronica's. I remember how proud she was the day she received *her* red blazer, how she stood in front of the mirror admiring herself in it."

Margaret and I smile sheepishly at each other; we'd both done the exact same thing.

Suddenly Ms. Harriman springs to her feet. "Let me show you Father's study. I think it will help you understand the next part of the story a little better."

We follow her down the hall and into a dark, musty

room. A pair of narrow stained glass windows (from a chapel in Rocamadour, France, I discover later) provide just enough light for me to see walls lined from floor to ceiling with shelves so jam-packed with books that there isn't enough room to slip in a comic book—or even a brochure. The furniture seems just right for an old archaeology professor—an impressive cherry desk and chairs with those creepy legs that look like a vulture's foot wrapped around a ball. Next to that is one of those overstuffed couches, the tuffet upon which Teazle sleeps soundly.

"This place is *great*," I say, running my hands reverently over the spines of the books.

Another confession: call me a geek if you must, but I just *love* books. I am absolutely obsessed with them. Go on, name any kids' book or series of books, and I probably have it. I spend so much of my allowance at the local bookstore that Margaret thinks I have some kind of a compulsive shopping disorder. Every time we get to the checkout line, me with an armful of books, she takes out her library card. Doesn't say a word, just holds it up right in front of my face and shakes her head sadly. Nothing against the library, but there's something different about having the book within reach when, say, I absolutely *need* to go back and reread that part in *Anne of Green Gables* that makes me cry every time I read it. (And speaking of books: if you're the person who borrowed my well-worn but much-loved hardcover copy of *The Secret Garden,* please return it—no questions asked.)

"Thank you," says Ms. Harriman. "His office at Columbia was even worse—or better, I suppose, depending on how you feel about books." She sits on the sofa next to Teazle and motions for us to sit, too. Winnie follows us into the study and sets another plate of blah cookies on a side table.

"Just in case," she says without a hint of a smile. And then she just kind of stands there.

"Thank you, Winifred. That's all for now." Ms. Harriman turns back to us. "I knew the second I met you that you could help me. And just seeing how you look at Father's book collection makes me even more certain."

Margaret gets right to the point. "Ms. Harriman, er, Elizabeth, I'm a little confused. We're just kids—how can we possibly help you?"

"By helping me find something." From a cream-colored envelope she takes out an ordinary-looking birthday card—the kind your grandparents send you, along with a check for ten dollars.

"Twenty years ago, Father bought this card for my daughter Caroline's fourteenth birthday. He wrote a short note inside, sealed the envelope, and then stuck it inside *The Complete Poems of Tennyson,* where it remained until yesterday, when I discovered it. He must have bought it a few days before her birthday and then hidden it from her—she was always snooping around his study—and then, to make a long story short, if that's still possible, he died."

"Oh my gosh, I'm so sorry," says Margaret.

"Oh, no, dear. Don't feel bad. It was a long time ago,

and my father really had a long, wonderful life. But, you see, inside this card there's a message for Caroline that I don't quite understand." She hands the card to Margaret. "Here, read what he said aloud so Sophie and Rebecca can hear."

Margaret reads:

December 9

My Dearest Caroline,

On the auspicious occasion of your fourteenth birthday, I present you with a very special gift— a gift of rare and precious beauty to match your own. A gift such as this one, however, demands that you must prove yourself worthy of possessing it, and so, in keeping with our mutual love of riddles and all things mysterious, I have created an elaborate puzzle for you: solve the puzzle, and you will find your gift.

You will find the first clue, as well as another note with more particulars, in the school library, within the only copy of our favorite play, Renidash's "Het Cholos orf Lanscad."

With all my love and best wishes
for a happy birthday,
Grandpa Ev

Margaret stares at the card for a few moments, smiling and shaking her head, and then hands it back to Ms. Harriman. "And you just found this?"

"That's right. He never gave it to her. He died on December 8, the day before her birthday. He was in that very chair when I found him." She points at the chair where I am sitting.

I squirm uncomfortably and try not to be *too* obvious as I remove my hands from the arms of the chair and set them in my lap, telling myself over and over not to freak out just because I am sitting where a guy died. Deep breaths, Sophie. Deep breaths.

"You think the other note might still be in that book at the school, don't you?" Margaret asks.

Ms. Harriman nods. "Not just the note. Everything."

"Everything?" Margaret says. "You mean, all the parts of the puzzle and the gift, too?"

"Exactly."

"Did he ever tell you what the gift is?" Rebecca asks.

She shakes her head. "I haven't the foggiest idea, but if he said it was—how did he put it—'rare and precious,' I'm inclined to think it may be something worth finding. Remember, he was an archaeologist. His business was finding rare and valuable old things."

"And this was hidden away in a book for twenty years," I marvel, pointing at the card.

"Serves me right for not being a fan of Tennyson," says Ms. Harriman with a sad smile. "I've always preferred Byron and Shelley."

"But a book in the school library is different. That's a *long* time for somebody to *not* stumble across it. And that's assuming the book is even still there," I say.

Margaret looks directly at me. "Well, we'll never know if we don't at least look."

That brings a satisfied smile to Ms. Harriman's red-as-my-blazer lips. "Do you really think you could look for it for me?"

"Wait, what about your daughter? Wouldn't she want to be involved in this? After all, it was her birthday, and it's her gift we would be looking for," Margaret says.

Ms. Harriman sighs deeply and sadly. "*That's* another story, and for that, I think we need more tea."

Winnie seems to materialize the second the word "tea" is mentioned.

"We'll take it in the living room," Ms. Harriman tells her.

I leap at the chance to get out of the dead-guy chair and return to the living room, where, over more tea and more cookies, Ms. Harriman tells us the story of her divorce from Malcolm and about her relationship—or actually, her complete *lack* of a relationship—with her daughter.

"After Father died, Malcolm and I began to drift apart. He continued the work Father started, traveling more and more, on long expeditions to the same places I had once spent so much time with Father. Malcolm never asked me to go along. But when Caroline started college, majoring in archaeology, she began to travel with him. I told myself that I didn't mind; by then I was very involved in the arts community here in the city, and I was certainly busy. But it did hurt, watching Caroline and Malcolm go off together—I felt like an outsider in my own family. By the time she started graduate school, Malcolm and I were divorced. I hardly ever saw Caroline; she spent two years outside of Istanbul, seeing Malcolm almost constantly and not once coming to New York to see me. The final straw came when I got a postcard from somewhere in Turkey informing me that she had married one of Malcolm's protégés—a British graduate student named Roger. Not that they were *getting* married, mind you. They *were* married. To add insult to injury, Malcolm had been there to give her away *and* act as best man in the wedding. I was so hurt and mad that I vowed never to speak to her again. About a year later, she had Caitlin, my granddaughter, whom I've never even seen."

I have a sudden urge to hug my mom. I don't think we've ever gone twelve hours without talking, and this lady hasn't spoken to her daughter in God knows how many *years*.

"They live overseas—or did, until a few months ago. Malcolm tells me that they have recently moved to the city, up in Washington Heights. Caroline is following in her grandfather's and father's footsteps and is teaching at Columbia."

"So your ex-husband never lost touch with Caroline?" Margaret asks.

"That's what he tells me. I see him once or twice a year and he gives me an update."

Margaret takes a deep breath. "But don't you want . . ."

Ms. Harriman smiles sadly. "Yes. No. I don't know. It's been so long. And now this," she says, holding up the birthday card and placing her hand over her heart.

Margaret looks first at Rebecca and then at me. "What do you think, guys? Up for a little adventure?"

"Always," I say.

"No problem," says Rebecca.

Margaret then copies the note exactly as it is written on the inside of the birthday card and hands the card back to Ms. Harriman. "Do you know anything about this play he mentions, *Het Cholos orf Lanscad* by Renidash? The title kind of sounds like it might be Latin, or maybe Greek, but I'm not so sure about the author's name. That doesn't sound familiar to me at all."

Ms. Harriman shakes her head. "I'm afraid I can't help you there. It doesn't ring any bells for me, either. My father, he was interested in so many things, and Caroline was exactly like him. They were always solving puzzles, or playing chess or backgammon, or reading some obscure poet. I used to feel a bit left out—maybe even a little jealous. From the time she was a little girl, I don't know why, but my daughter and I never seemed to have enough in common."

"Can you tell us a little more about what she was like

at the time this letter was written?" Margaret asks. "What kind of things did she like to read? What else was she into? You know, like fashion, or photography, dance, whatever. What did she want to be? Anything that might help us with this first clue."

Ms. Harriman ponders this for a second. "What did she read? Anything, everything. She wanted to be an actress. More than anything. She was the lead in several plays at the school: Juliet in *Romeo and Juliet,* Emily in *Our Town.*"

"That's my absolute favorite play," I gush.

"Mine too," Ms. Harriman agrees. "Although I haven't been able to see it, or even read it since Caroline—it hits a little too close to home, if you know what I mean. And I almost forgot—she played the violin."

"Me too!" says Margaret, who is Mom's star pupil and part of the reason I switched to the guitar a couple of years ago. (She was playing Bach and Mozart when I was still scratching away at "Twinkle, Twinkle, Little Star" while Mom winced encouragingly.)

"Caroline was like that Schroeder character in the *Peanuts* cartoon—she just *loved* her Beethoven. I really miss her music. Margaret, maybe you and Sophie can play for me sometime."

Quick, change the subject before Margaret agrees to some wacky violin-guitar duet. "Do you have a picture of Caroline? I don't know why, but I think it might help, just knowing what she looked like."

Without a word, Ms. Harriman goes to a table behind the sofa and gently lifts a framed photograph from it, cradling it in her hands as if it were her most precious possession—and perhaps it is? "This is Caroline with my father, and her new kitten, on her thirteenth birthday." She hands the frame to me. "That tiny kitten, believe it or not, is Teazle. He was a gift from my father. Twenty-one years old and still going strong." Teazle lifts his head briefly at the sound of his name.

"She's beautiful," says Margaret. "Your daughter, I mean. Not the cat. Not that he's not beautiful, too," she adds, very Margaret-like, for Teazle's sake.

Everything about this girl in the photograph seems perfect, and suddenly I am overwhelmed with sadness. I hand the frame back to Ms. Harriman without looking her in the eye. "Thank you. It's nice to have a face to go with the name."

We start to head for the door.

"Girls, thank you. Thank you for listening, and for offering to help."

"We'll let you know as soon as we find anything," Margaret says.

"If," I say, half under my breath.

"When!" Margaret corrects.

And *that,* gentle reader, is how the Red Blazer Girls got their very first case.

Chapter 3

In which I play fast and loose with the English language and we add a recruit to our ranks

All the way home on the subway that afternoon, as Margaret chatters about Ms. Harriman, the note, and our one clue, I can't stop thinking about that girl in the photograph. It is hard for me to process that that amazing-looking girl, confidently posed in her red blazer, is now almost thirty-four years old and has a daughter of her own who is practically our age. And the man she is standing next to, looking at with such love, has been dead for twenty years. I have never even met these people, but I am almost in tears thinking about them. And then there is Caroline's father, Ms. Harriman's ex-husband. She had said his name was Malcolm Chance. Mal Chance. *Mal chance*. That's, well, French for "bad luck." In addition to hugging my mom when I get home, I resolve to call all my grandparents, even Great-grandmère Henrietta in France, which is always a bit of a linguistic adventure.

I lock myself in my room and make it through the first ten chapters of *Great Expectations*. It isn't too bad. ("Isn't too bad!" Mr. E cries, clutching his chest in a mock heart attack when I make that very observation in class the next day. "It's Charles Dickens, for crying out *loud*.") This is my first real Dickens experience, and I am pleasantly surprised at how funny it is. There's this line about Mrs. Joe raising Pip "by hand"—meaning she smacks him a *lot*—and that part where Pumblechook thinks the tar water he's drinking is brandy has me laughing out loud. So, though I'm still not sure it's the "greatest novel ever," I am definitely getting into it.

After I set Mr. Dickens aside, I resist the urge to go online and dig out my math book. By nine-fifteen, totally confused and desperate for help, I IM Margaret.

> **Sophie:** M did u get 5???? Help!!!
> **Margaret:** Soph, you're kidding, right? That's the easiest problem of the bunch. Wow, this is such a George and Emily moment.
> **Sophie:** what ru talking about?
> **Margaret:** Our Town. George and Emily. Remember?

George Gibbs. Emily Webb. *Our Town*. She means the scene where George and Emily, who are next-door neighbors, are talking from their bedroom windows.

Emily, the "smartest girl in school," is helping poor, dim George with what seems to be a pretty simple algebra problem. I'm pretty sure I've just been insulted.

> **Margaret:** A hint. The answer is in square yards of wallpaper.

Exactly what Emily tells George.

> **Sophie:** biteme
> **Margaret:** If you want my help, you're going to have to improve your manners. That kind of language is wildly inappropriate.
> **Sophie:** ok sister margaret manners ill try pleasepleasepleasehelphelphelpme
> **Margaret:** Much better. Now, if you know that angle B is 65 degrees, what does that tell you about angle C?

Oh, good Lord. A monkey could solve it.

> **Sophie:** ur right im an idiot ☹
> **Margaret:** I never said that. Soph, I've been thinking. This thing with Elizabeth, we should tell Leigh Ann, too. Let her in the club.
> **Sophie:** really? why?

Leigh Ann transferred to St. Veronica's from another girls' school and we are just getting to know her. She seems nice enough, I guess.

Margaret: Because she's really smart, and nice, and funny, and sweet. Give her a chance— she'll fit in perfectly.
Sophie: ok i guess but i like my old friends best

A few moments later, Rebecca calls.

"Did you get number five in the math homework?" she asks.

"Only after Margaret gave me a hint."

"What was the hint?"

"Look at angle B—it's sixty-five degrees, right?"

"Uh-huh."

"So . . ."

"So what?"

"So angle C *has* to be what?"

"Ohhhhh. That *is* easy. Thanks."

"No problemo. Hey, Becca—what do you think of Leigh Ann? Margaret thinks we should, you know, let her into the club."

"We have a club? I dunno. She seems okay. Beautiful, that's for sure. And kind of brainy. Is she as smart as Margaret?"

"Is *anybody* as smart as Margaret?"

"Good point. Oh, Soph, you know that Dickens thing you guys talked me into?"

Every fall, Mr. Eliot hosts this wacky event he calls "A Dickens of a Banquet." He dresses up like Charles

Dickens and reads from his favorite novels, and the cafeteria ladies serve a traditional old-fashioned English meal of roast beef and Yorkshire pudding, and Brussels sprouts, and something rumored to be fig pudding for dessert. (My dad raised a suspicious French eyebrow when I explained the concept of the Dickens banquet. "An *English* feast? I think not.") Parents and other adults have to pay, but students get to eat for free. There's a catch, however: if you want to eat, you have to perform. You can go it alone with a reading or a monologue, or, for the slightly more adventurous, a group of students can write and perform a skit based on a scene from a Dickens story. Margaret, Leigh Ann, and I are in Mr. Eliot's honors English class, and Leigh Ann, who loves to perform, talked us into doing a skit with her. We recruited Rebecca and decided to adapt a scene from *Great Expectations,* since we had to read the book anyway.

"Yeah, what about the banquet?"

"I don't know if I'm going to be able to do it with you guys."

"What? Why?"

"Because after tomorrow, I'm going to have to start going straight home after school, and I doubt that you guys want to schlep down to Chinatown every time you want to practice."

"Why do you have to go straight home?"

"To babysit my brother and sister."

"I thought your mom was working the night shift. Isn't she home in the afternoon?"

"Well, she *was,* but things have changed. As of next month, it looks like she's out of a job, and who knows what's going to happen to us. If she doesn't find a job right away, I'm probably going to have to leave the school. Tuition for three of us—there's no way we can afford that."

"I'm sure she'll get another job. Your mom is awesome. And can't you talk to Sister Bernadette about financial aid? There must be something the school can do."

"I already get half my tuition paid from a scholarship, but that runs out this year. Next year, I'll have to pay the whole thing, and there's no way, even if the school comes up with some of the money."

"Rebecca, you *cannot* leave St. V's."

"Believe me, Soph, just the thought of not being with my girls . . . hey, I have to finish my homework. And, Soph?"

"Yeah?"

"Please don't say anything to anybody. And look, don't worry about it. It's not your problem."

But I *am* worried. I love our perfect trio. No Rebecca? Unthinkable!

Margaret calls me on my cell the next morning—at *six o'clock.*

"What."

"Good morning, darling sunshine. Did I wake you?" She actually giggles.

I glance out my window. "It's still dark outside! For Pete's sake, Margaret! Don't you dare be cheerful."

"Oh, c'mon, just get up. I'll be at your building in eleven minutes," she says.

Not ten minutes. Not twelve minutes.

"I want us to be there when the school opens. Mr. Eliot always comes in early. He can let us into the library, right? Sophie, are you up yet?"

"I'm up, I'm up," I lie, I lie.

"We'll stop at Perkatory; my treat."

"I'm ordering something very expensive."

Just around the corner from the church is Perkatory, a favorite coffeehouse/hangout for St. Veronica's girls (and some teachers). The entrance is a few steps down from the street—not quite aboveground, not quite below, hence the name. Like *purgatory,* get it? When we go inside, Mr. Eliot is seated at a rickety café table with his coffee, a *pain au chocolat* (yum!), and the *New York Times*. He looks up at us and then at his watch. A strange expression crosses his face.

"I'll take a large, no, make that an *extra*-large hot chocolate. And can I have one of those?" I say, pointing at Mr. Eliot's pastry. *"S'il vous plaît."* I drop my backpack and slump into a chair, laying my head on the table.

A few minutes later, a disgustingly cheerful Margaret sits down with our hot chocolates and pastries. "So, did you tell him yet?"

Mr. Eliot lowers his paper a few inches and raises his eyebrows.

"You might be interested to know that Sophie was right," Margaret says.

"Sophie St. Pierre? My God, what are the odds?"

"Hey, she *did* see something yesterday."

"Ah, the scream."

"Exactly. The *valid* scream."

Margaret spills about everything, including the part where we snuck out of school. "And after school, we went over to her house."

"Was she wearing a tattered, yellowing wedding dress? Did she invite you in to play cards with an ill-tempered girl named Estella?"

"As a matter of fact," I say, lifting my head from the table, "she was *not* wearing a wedding dress, she had both shoes on, the clocks were not all stopped at twenty minutes to nine, and her name is Ms. *Harriman,* not Havisham."

Mr. Eliot grins. "Glad to see that you've been reading your Dickens."

"There was no Estella or Mr. Jaggers, but there *was* a Caroline," Margaret adds. "Which is why we're here." The rest of our escapade leaves him shaking his head.

"That is one heckuva story."

"It is pretty cool, huh?" I know he is more interested

than he's letting on; he has folded his paper and set it aside so he can devote all his attention.

"As a responsible adult," he says, "I *should* be really angry with you. You meet some random woman in a 'secret passageway' in the church, and without a second thought, you go right in her house. She could've been an ax murderer."

"Oh, don't be so dramatic, Mr. Eliot," Margaret says. "Jeez, give us a little credit. We're city girls—we've got street smarts and all that."

"On the other hand," he continues, "I have to tell you: I wish to God I'd been there with you. The whole thing is positively Dickensian! The long-lost birthday card with the mysterious clue, the strange voice on the telephone, the estranged daughter who marries the foreigner, the twenty-year-old giant cat, the walls covered in masterpieces. I can't wait to hear what happens next!"

With that, Margaret hands him his briefcase and pushes him toward the door. "I am happy to hear you say that, Mr. Eliot. Because *you* are going to help us decipher our first clue."

Chapter 4

In which a small piece of the past comes to light, and we learn the shocking family secret that William Shakespeare doesn't want you to know!

"I'll give you half an hour," Mr. Eliot says as we make our way from Perkatory to the school. "Just be out of the library before Mrs. Overmeyer gets in. School librarians are *very* territorial. And no snooping around her desk or on her computer."

"Yes, sir, Mr. Eliot, sir!" Such mistrust!

Margaret has already determined which years we are looking for, so we go straight to the shelf where all the old yearbooks sit, collecting dust.

She pulls one out and blows dust off the cover. "This should be her freshman year."

"What are we looking for, anyway?"

"We need to see her in her environment—see what else we can learn about her. I can't figure out this *Het Cholos orf Lanscad* thing. I looked online, but there was nothing about it or a writer named Renidash. Here, you take her sophomore year and see what you can find."

I start leafing through the book at one of the library tables, its wooden top pocked with decades of student scratching and graffiti.

"Hey, here she is, in this picture of the Drama Club," Margaret says. " 'Caroline Chance was our Juliet.' God, she *was* beautiful, and jeez, a freshman with the lead in *Romeo and Juliet*? Don't tell Leigh Ann, but I'm not so sure even *she's* ready for that kind of part. How about yours? Find anything?"

"Think so." I turn Margaret's attention to the inside back cover of the yearbook I am holding. "It says: 'To Mrs. Overmeyer, Thanks for all the terrific book recommendations and for all your help with my Brit Lit project. Who knows, maybe together we'll make RBS popular again! Enjoy your summer in Ireland, away from our own little School for Scandal. All the best, Caroline Chance.' "

"I'm sure Mrs. Overmeyer will remember her," Margaret says. "It sounds like they knew each other pretty well. I wonder what RBS is."

"Sounds like a TV station. You know, like PBS."

"Hey, that's not bad, Soph. You're wrong, unfortunately, but at least you're getting into the spirit of things."

"Nancy Drew! Harriet! What are *you* girls doing in here!" Mr. Eliot barges through the library door, trying (and failing) to scare us with this really fake-angry voice.

Margaret holds out the yearbook to him. "Hey, Mr. E, take a look at this."

He reads the inscription and grunts. "Hm. I'm not surprised that Mrs. Overmeyer knew her. She's been here forever. How long ago was this, almost twenty years? There are still a couple of other teachers who were here then, besides Mrs. Overmeyer. But seriously, how is this helpful?"

Margaret, a tiny bit indignant at his attitude, slams the book shut. "Well, we don't know, *yet.*"

"Okay, Miss Marple, but right now you need to move it on out of here. You can talk to Mrs. Overmeyer later."

As Margaret and I follow him to his classroom, I ask him if he has any ideas about the reference to RBS in the yearbook.

"Sure. Randy Bob Shakespeare. RBS. Will's younger brother. A real redneck. Specialized in plays about Elizabethan trailer parks."

"Mr. Eliot, why can't you ever just admit there's stuff you don't know?"

"Oh, he knows what it is," said Margaret.

Mr. Eliot smiles.

"And you're not going to tell us!"

"C'mon, wouldn't you rather figure it out on your own? Tell you what—if you don't have it by the end of the day, come and see me. I'll give you a little hint: she capitalized *school* and *scandal.* You're the detectives—detect!"

I *am* starting to feel like a detective, but first I have to go to math class.

Chapter 5

In which Margaret declares herself to be a moron, causing me to wonder what that would make me

After math class, I totally bomb a Spanish quiz (since I already speak French fluently, they make me take Spanish—*c'est injuste!*) and I'm pretty sure I dozed off in religion class (Lord, please forgive me!), so I am really looking forward to lunch. Leigh Ann joins our table for the first time, and over French fries and chicken nuggets, we tell her all about our little adventure. She is properly impressed and really excited that we have included her. (I'm still a bit doubtful about the whole quartet thing.) After dumping our trays, we all head back to the library to continue our research. Mrs. Overmeyer is on the phone when we get there, so Margaret immediately heads for one of the computers and logs on. Margaret is smart, *not* patient.

She types in "school for scandal," and we wait. When the results pop up, her mouth opens so wide her chin almost hits the table. "Oh my God. Turns out I am a complete moron. Sophie, do you have the note?"

I pull it out of my bag and hand it to her.

Margaret pounds the heel of her hand against her forehead. "I repeat—a moron." She shoves the note under our noses, and we all try to see what had suddenly become so clear to her. "Do you see it?"

"Uh, no," I say.

"Look at the note again. He talks about this play, Renidash's *Het Cholos orf Lanscad*. Look at what I found when I looked under 'School for Scandal.' It was written by Richard Brinsley Sheridan. RBS. Now, look at the names again: *Sheridan. Renidash.*"

"Ahhhh. I see it. The letters are all jumbled up," I say.

"An anagram," says Margaret.

"And *Het Cholos orf Lanscad* is *School for Scandal*!" notes Leigh Ann, jumping right into the thick of things.

"That Professor Harriman was a clever little man, wasn't he?" I say. "So, what is this *School for Scandal*, anyway?"

Margaret scrolls down the screen. "Let's see. It's a play. Oh my God, it's in the Harvard Classics! It's in volume eighteen, *Modern English Drama*."

"Have you read it?" I ask. "What's it about?"

"Not yet. It says here it is a 'comedy of manners.' "

Rebecca has a puzzled look. "A play about manners? Is that like 'Don't talk with your mouth full'? How do you turn that into a play?"

"It's about a gossipy woman named—oh, Mr. Eliot

would love this name—Lady Sneerwell, and hey, wait a minute, remember the cat?"

"Teaser," I say.

"*Teazle,*" Margaret corrects. "There's a character named Lady Teazle. Let's see if it's still here in the library." She leaps out of her seat to go to the card catalog computer and types in the name of the play. "Oh, no. It's in storage." She lets that sink in for a second before starting her rant. "Wait a minute. The Harvard Classics are in *storage*? What kind of school is this? What kind of world are we living in? I have to talk to Mrs. Overmeyer." She marches over to the librarian's desk, arriving as Mrs. Overmeyer hangs up the phone.

"Yes, de-ah. How might I be of service to ye?" she asks. After something like forty-five years in the States, her Irish accent is as thick as day-old oatmeal.

"If a book is in storage, where would I find it?" Margaret asks.

"Oh de-ah. As the late Mr. Overmeyer—God rest his soul—would have said, 'Are ye feeling lucky?' The truth is, it depends. What are you looking for? Maybe you can find the full text online. The Internet is wonderful that way."

"No, I'm afraid I need the actual book. It's a play, part of the Harvard Classics, called *The School for Scandal.*"

Mrs. Overmeyer's face brightens instantly. "My word. No one's asked for that since—"

"It's by—"

"Yes, I know. Sheridan. Richard Brinsley Sheridan. He was born in me hometown of Dublin. Not too many people reading him these days. Are you interested in him? Or just that play in particular?"

"Well, both, kind of. But mostly that play. Do you know where it is?"

"Well, *if* we still have it—that is, if it didn't get ruined when the basement flooded a few years back—and if it didn't get tossed out by someone else, then it would still be in the storage area in the basement. When do you need it?"

"Now-ish?"

"Well, if you really need it in a hurry, my best advice is to head for the public library on Sixty-seventh, between First and Second. They can get it for you." Mrs. Overmeyer sees the disappointment on our faces and adds, "I'm sorry, but I'm not allowed to let you into the storage area by yourselves. Sister Bernadette would hang me by me thumbs."

"What if a teacher went with us?" I know just who to ask.

"If you can find a teacher to go down in that godforsaken place and help you look for a moldy old book, then God love ye. Might I ask why it's so important that you find *that* book?"

"Mrs. Overmeyer," Margaret begins, leaning over the counter, "do you remember a girl named Caroline Chance? She would have been here—"

"Of course I remember Miss Chance. It must be ten, no, more than that, must be fifteen years or more since she was here." She has a quizzical look on her face. "Why do you ask?"

Margaret and I look at each other, unsure of how much to reveal. "We met someone, someone who—who used to know her," Margaret says. "And she asked us to do a favor for her."

"Her mother?"

"How did you know?"

"Just a hunch. I see her around every now and again. 'Tis a shame about her and Caroline."

"So you know all about the—"

Mrs. Overmeyer nods. "Sure, I know about them. The family was very closely connected to St. Veronica's— Caroline's grandfather was on the board for many years before he passed on, and her father, Mr. Malcolm Chance, still is. Is this book you're looking for somehow related to this favor ye mentioned?"

"Kind of," Margaret says. "We're looking for something, but without really knowing what we're looking for."

"And we saw that she had signed your yearbook," I add, pointing to the shelf where the book rested. "She said something about how you had helped her with a lit project, and something else about RBS and *The School for Scandal*."

"We just want to see it, to see if she, I don't know, wrote something in the margin or something. We're just, uh, curious. So, it's okay if we go down to the basement to look for it, as long as we have a teacher with us?"

"It's okay with me, girls," she says with a condescending smile, "but I wouldn't bet me teeth on finding anything."

We are *always* being underestimated.

Chapter 6

In which Otto Frank provides moral guidance, and mold spores are redeemed

It is a book we are looking for, after all, and Mr. Eliot loves books *almost* as much as I do. Well, there's that and the fact that we weren't going to leave him alone until he agreed. And so he's now leading the way into the dimly lit, hot, funky-smelling basement, piled from floor to ceiling with rapidly disintegrating cartons of God-knows-what. There are twenty-five or thirty cartons, all of about the same size and vintage, and none of them have labels. We're just going to have to dig in.

Twenty minutes later, a dust-covered Mr. Eliot shouts, "Eureka! The Harvard Classics," and holds up a green, slightly moldy leather-bound book as proof of his discovery. "Volume thirty-three, *Voyages and Travels.*"

Margaret, Rebecca, and I pounce on the box, elbows flying as we pull the books out one by one while Leigh Ann looks on in wonder, not quite sure what she has gotten herself into.

"Thirty-one. Thirty-seven. Forty-five. Forty-four. Eleven. Twelve, seventeen, EIGHTEEN!" Margaret announces. *"Modern English Drama."* She hugs it to her chest. Unlike the others, this volume is still wearing its plastic, standard library-issue dust cover, brittle and yellowed with age, and held in place by even yellower cellophane tape.

"The moment of truth, ladies and gentlemen." Mr. Eliot imitates a drumroll. "Spotlight, please."

"Aw, just open it."

Slowly, cautiously, as if she is afraid a snake is going to pop out of it, Margaret lifts the cover. Her eyes brighten, and her lips curl into an ever-so-slight smile. "Oh, my."

"What? Let me see," I say, anxious.

She holds the open book before us. Tucked inside the cover of volume eighteen of the Harvard Classics is another cream-colored envelope, exactly like the one that contained the birthday card! Written in Everett Harriman's distinctive cursive is the name Caroline.

"Hmmm. The adventure continues. Is this—" Mr. Eliot starts, holding up the envelope.

"Exactly what we are looking for?" Margaret finishes. "Yes, I believe it is." She takes the book in her hands and begins to leaf through the pages.

"Oh my God," I say. "What if there's a map in there directing her to like a million dollars or something?"

"Yeah! We could be stinkin' rich. Mwha-ha-ha!"

Rebecca laughs maniacally as Leigh Ann wisely backs away.

"Whatever is in that envelope belongs to your Ms. Harriman or to her daughter, not to you," Mr. Eliot pointedly reminds her.

"Who's to know?" Rebecca responds. "There are no live witnesses—unless you count the mold."

"What about me?" Mr. Eliot asks. "How are you going to keep me from talking, Mr. Poe? Shackle me in chains and build a brick wall around me?"

"Oh, lighten up, Mr. E! And who's Mr. Poe?"

"As in Edgar Allan, you dope," says Margaret, placing the envelope back inside the book. "He wrote 'The Cask of Amontillado,' the story he's referring to. And we're not even going to open this envelope until we get to Ms. Harriman's."

"My first and only chance for easy money, cruelly dashed by an honest friend—and a teacher who calls me mister."

Leigh Ann shakes her head in disbelief. "I'm just amazed that the envelope is still there. All that time, and not *one* person checked out, or even opened, that book."

"I know. And it's a Harvard Classic." Margaret looks inside the cover at the pocket where the old checkout card rests, undisturbed for so many years. "This book has been in the library for almost fifty years, and it has been checked out exactly once."

"Are you sure we can't take a peek at what's inside

the envelope now?" Leigh Ann asks. "I mean, aren't you *dying* of curiosity?"

"Think of it like Anne Frank's diary; it's a . . ." I pause, searching for the right words. "It's a relic, a historical document. We owe it to future generations! It should be read. No, it MUST be read!"

Mr. Eliot will have none of it. "Nice try, Sophie, but remember, it was Otto Frank, Anne's father, who made the decision to publish the diary. Not a bunch of strangers."

We start to leave, but stop when Mr. Eliot clears his throat.

"Ladies, are you forgetting something?"

We look around the ransacked boxes, expecting to see a book bag or something else that one of us is about to leave behind.

"The books, ladies. We're going to leave them just the way we found them." He looks at the carton containing the Harvard Classics and shakes his head. "This really is a shame, having these wonderful books hidden away, rotting. I can't believe they can't find any room for them upstairs."

"You have space in your bookcases," Leigh Ann suggests.

"Hmmm. Maybe I do. Okay, leave the mess for now. Let's get out of here before we all end up with the bubonic plague or something from breathing in all these mold spores."

"The plague was spread by fleas," says Encyclopedia Margaret.

"I was trying to make a point. I *know* what caused the plague."

Teachers. They are *so* sensitive if you even suggest that they don't *always* know what they're talking about. Which they *don't*!

Chapter 7

In which I vow not to complain about the card and $10 my grandfather sends me for my birthday

"We found it!" I blurt out the second Ms. Harriman opens her bright red door, looking a little frightened by my exuberant greeting. Dad says my rashness comes from Mom's side of the gene pool and that his side is far more refined.

"Goodness! That was certainly fast work!" Ms. Harriman ushers us in the door and into the foyer, where, surprisingly, an elegantly dressed man stands, smiling.

"My, my," he says as the four of us crowd into the foyer. "Here's a sight I haven't seen in this house for more years than I care to admit—a veritable gaggle of gregarious girls in red blazers. Once upon a time, this was a fairly common sight in here, wasn't it, Elizabeth?"

Margaret stops in her tracks, holding the book tight to her chest. "Sorry. We didn't realize you had company. We can just come back tomorrow."

"No, no, please," says the man, who looks like one of those English country gentlemen from a PBS series— well over six feet tall, with a full head of thick, slicked-back black hair, a bushy mustache that covers most of his mouth, and about half an acre of tweed. He even has a carved walking stick, as if he is just back from a stroll on his Welsh estate. But still, here's the thing: something about him feels "off" and kind of creepy. His accent sounds like someone *pretending* to be British, and he has an odd odor—not cologne or soap. I can't quite place it.

He insists that he is on his way out and that we should stay. Ms. Harriman looks like she isn't sure whether to introduce us or not, but I've noticed that with people her age, manners always seem to get the best of them.

"Girls, this is Mr. Chance. Excuse me, that's *Doctor* Malcolm Chance. And this is Margaret and Sophie, and Rebecca, and—I'm afraid I haven't met your other friend." She holds out her hand to Leigh Ann.

"Oh, I'm sorry—this is our friend Leigh Ann Jaimes," says Margaret, embarrassed at her breach of etiquette.

"Elizabeth Harriman. So nice to meet you. Malcolm, these girls are doing a little research project for me."

"Ahhhh. Interesting. And apparently successful," he says with a glance at me (and my big mouth). "Well, I will bid you all farewell and allow you to continue your report. Good-bye, Elizabeth. I will *definitely* be in touch. And Winifred, *always* a pleasure."

Jeez, I hadn't even realized it, but that Winifred is standing about six inches behind me, glaring over my shoulder at Malcolm as he bows dramatically and exits.

Ms. Harriman closes and locks the door and starts to move back toward us. Suddenly, though, she stops in her tracks, turns back, and lets loose an old-fashioned "Bronx cheer," a spitty, farty sound, along with the traditional dismissive wave of the hand. Seeing the slightly shocked expressions on our faces, she says, "Oh, I'm sorry, girls. That wasn't exactly the proper thing to do, but that man, he always gets my goat."

"He is—"

"My ex-husband. Who still lives uncomfortably close by."

"Have you told him about the birthday card?" Margaret asks.

"Oh, goodness no. And I don't intend to. At least, not now. I'm not sure why he stopped by. He said he was 'in the neighborhood' and thought he would 'check up' on me. Trust me, Malcolm has never checked up on me or anyone. He's snooping around for something, I'm sure. Well, anyway, enough about him. You found something? Wonderful! Please, come inside and sit, and tell me all about it."

On the way into the living room, Leigh Ann grabs my arm and pulls me aside. "You didn't tell me she was crazy."

"Do you really think she's crazy?"

"Are you kidding me? *What* is she wearing? Is that a wedding dress?"

"Nah, it's just a long white dress. With buckles. And fringe. And matching cowboy boots. An odd choice, I'll admit, especially for November, but definitely not a wedding dress." My otherwise modern mom insists that one simply does *not* wear white after Labor Day.

We take our seats in the living room, and as Winifred brings us more tea and cookies, Margaret leads Ms. Harriman through our basement adventure. Then she opens the book with a triumphant flourish and holds out the envelope to her. "Do you recognize the handwriting?"

Ms. Harriman takes the envelope in her hands, holding it gingerly, seemingly afraid to touch it. "Father's writing. Oh my goodness. I don't know what to say, girls." Her hands are shaking and her eyes water as she caresses the envelope, running her finger over the script. It's hard not to feel sorry for her.

"We didn't read it," I assure her.

Ms. Harriman smiles at that. "That's very kind of you, but it would have been all right if you had. I trust you girls."

Okay. Very nice. Touching, even. But if *someone* doesn't open that stupid envelope in the next ten seconds, I am going to explode. Ms. Harriman picks up a mother-of-pearl-handled letter opener from the desk and slices the envelope open. She pulls out a folded note card embossed with the initials EMH and reads:

My Dearest Caroline,

Well done! I was certain that a simple anagram wouldn't even slow you down.

As promised, this continues your birthday gift with a puzzle for you to solve:

$$(i) + (ii) = (iii)$$

$$(iv) - (v) = (vi)$$

Each of the Roman numerals in the above equations corresponds to a clue. For each clue that you solve, another will be provided. The solution to the puzzle will lead you to the gift.

A hint: all of the clues except the last refer to objects or places in or on the church.

A little background information: the object of your treasure hunt truly is a "treasure," one of a pair of such objects. The other is in the Metropolitan Museum of Art, a gift to the museum from my friend and mentor, Zoltan Ressanyi.

I am confident that your knowledge of religion, classical languages, mathematics, literature, philosophy, and art is up to the challenge of solving the puzzle and finding the treasure. Happy hunting, and remember —sometimes in life the most difficult problems are solved by lying in bed and staring at that seemingly insignificant fly on the ceiling.

And now, your first clue (for "i"):
Look behind LQ324

Happy hunting!
Love,
Grandpa Ev

Chapter 8

In which I determine that King Tut lives in the blue pyramid and smokes unfiltered Camels

The shiny wheels in Margaret's brain are whizzing at maximum speed by the time Ms. Harriman finishes reading the letter.

"Does this make any sense at all to you?" she asks.

Ms. Harriman is indeed a portrait of confusion as she reads the note over again to herself. "Well, I certainly remember Professor Ressanyi. He was a famous archaeologist. I believe he was with Howard Carter when they opened the tomb of Tutankhamen in 1922, but his area of expertise, like Father's, was early Christian artifacts. And this puzzle, these clues . . . I can tell you that both Father and Caroline loved brain teasers, logic problems, crosswords, anagrams—puzzles of any kind. But the treasure part, well . . ."

Ms. Harriman pauses for a second too long, and Margaret jumps in. "Is there something else we should know about this?"

"Well, I was just remembering something that happened after Father passed away. His original will mentioned an item of some value that he had intended to go to the Metropolitan Museum—a ring, I believe, from somewhere in France—and gave its location as a case he kept in his office at the university. When we went to find it, however, we found in its place a codicil to his will—a change he made a few days before he died, in which he deleted that one particular gift. No other changes to the will. At the time, we didn't think too much of it. We simply assumed that he had done something else with it; he was always donating items to various museums, university collections, and such around the country. But now that I think of it, Malcolm knew about this ring and where Father kept it, and he was certain that Father hadn't given it away."

"Maybe he knew that your father planned to give it to Caroline?" Margaret suggests.

"An interesting idea, Margaret," says Ms. Harriman.

"Ohmigosh, did you see the way he looked at me when I said 'We found it'?" I say. "I wonder if he thinks *that's* what we found."

"With Malcolm, anything's possible. I'm sure he would love to have it—especially if it is something important or that could advance his career. Pompous old twit."

Leigh Ann, sitting next to me on the couch, elbows me. I try to ignore her because I am listening to Ms.

Harriman, and I am also a little afraid that she is going to make me laugh. She elbows me again, harder.

"What?" I hiss.

"Don't turn around," she says, under her breath, "but that housekeeper lady is spying on us."

"Where?" I start to turn my head.

"*Don't* look! I can see her in that mirror over by the stairs. She is totally snooping."

I scooch over on the couch in order to get the same angle Leigh Ann has, and sure enough, there is Winifred, standing behind a pillar at the entrance to the living room, her head cocked in a classic eavesdropping pose.

"See?"

"I sure do."

"What should we do?"

New to this world of spies and secrets, I can only come up with: "Dunno."

"About this letter," Margaret continues. "Do you want us to start trying to solve the puzzle, just in case the ring is still where your father left it?"

"Well, you certainly have a better chance of finding it than I do. Heavens, I'm outfoxed by simple crossword puzzles. I wouldn't have the foggiest notion of where to begin."

"It's like the first time you read a word problem in algebra. It makes no sense," I say, keeping one eye on Winifred. "But after a few minutes, you start to see it.

It's the same thing with those goofy logic problems. You know, the ones where they tell you that Aaron smokes Lucky Strikes, and Betty lives in a green house, and Cameron lives next door to Aaron, so then who drives a red Ford? It always *seems* like they haven't given you enough information, but when you sit down and organize it, there always is *just* enough to solve it, and you figure out that Doug quit smoking and lives between Betty and Cameron and drives a purple Chevrolet." I take a much-needed breath and point at the letter. "This is just like that."

"But when I look at that clue, and those equations or whatever they are, I don't see how they can tell us where something is hidden," Margaret says.

I take a peek in the mirror and see Winifred still in position, straining to hear every word. I then turn to Ms. Harriman. "Obviously, Caroline was really brainy, right? And your father was a professor at Columbia. And it sounds like he was pretty sure that she could figure it out, based on what she knew. I mean, she was almost the same age as us—okay, a couple years older. But c'mon, Margaret, how much more could she know? What about all those books you read? Don't they count for anything?" (I'm on a roll.) "Look how fast you found this envelope. It took you like five minutes to figure that one out. I'd still be in the library, flailing through the shelves. So, what do you think?"

The fortunate combination of her own insatiable

curiosity and my unique ability to be a royal pain in her butt wears her down.

"You actually trust us to do this?" she asks Ms. Harriman.

Ms. Harriman laughs. "I do trust you. All I ask is that you keep this between us."

"And Mr. Eliot, our English teacher," I say. "He helped us find the book, so he knows a little already. But he's cool; he'll keep it secret if we ask."

"Well, then. I guess you girls have another puzzle to solve."

Back in the foyer, we are saying our good-byes when Ms. Harriman points to Rebecca's ever-present sketch-pad. "I noticed that you did some sketching while we were chatting."

"Yeah, I'm sorry," Rebecca says. "I don't mean to be rude. Sometimes I don't even realize I'm doing it."

"Okay if I take a quick peek?"

Rebecca instinctively hugs the pad closer to her body but then slowly relaxes her death grip as we start to hound her. "Um, okay."

Ms. Harriman opens it very carefully, turning the pages as if each holds a masterpiece. "Rebecca, dear, these are quite remarkable."

"Told you she was good," I say.

"Well, you were only being accurate." She pauses, staring at a drawing of the famous Bethesda Fountain in Central Park, her fingers hovering over the delicate pencil lines. "Gracious." She turns a few more pages, stopping at a page filled with a number of smaller drawings—the very ones Rebecca had been working on a few minutes earlier.

"Oh, those are just—" Rebecca starts, trying to close the pad.

"Why, that's me," says Ms. Harriman. "And there's Winifred. And Margaret. Goodness, Rebecca, you have a gift. Have you had any formal training?"

"N-no. I mean, just some art classes at school."

"My dear, there is someone I *must* introduce you to. What are you doing Saturday afternoon?"

"Um . . . babysitting, probably. My brother and sister."

"Well, I'll tell you what," Ms. Harriman says, moving to a small table arranged with stationery and a gold-tipped fountain pen. She writes down an address and hands it to Rebecca. "This is the address of a gallery in Chelsea, owned by a very good friend. I would love for her to see your work and for you to talk to her. She loves to help budding young artists, and I'm sure she'll have some good advice for you. I'm meeting her there at two-thirty—please try to make it. Bring your sketchbook and anything else you've done."

Now we are all gathered around Rebecca, staring and making her completely squirmy. She backs away. "I—I'll try, but I—"

"Jeez, Becca, *I'll* watch your brother and sister for you, if that's the problem. You have to go."

"I'll be there."

"Wonderful!" Ms. Harriman smiles. "Saturday, then."

The second the red door to Ms. Harriman's closes behind us, Leigh Ann and I are both right in Margaret's face.

"Did you see her?" Leigh Ann asks.

"See who? What are you talking about?"

"Winifred," I say. "The housekeeper—"

"—spying on us!" Leigh Ann exclaims.

"Spying? Are you sure?"

"Completely," I say. "It was totally obvious. She was hiding behind one of those pillars, but we could see her in the mirror."

Margaret is skeptical. "Rebecca, did you see anything?"

"Rebecca couldn't see her where she was sitting."

"You're sure she was eavesdropping and not just waiting for Ms. Harriman to ask for more tea or something?"

Leigh Ann and I look at each other, shaking our heads emphatically.

"Definitely snooping," I say.

"Well, that makes two interesting . . . occurrences involving Winifred," Margaret says. "We will have to keep our eyes and ears open."

Hmmmmm. A twist on the old "the butler did it" theory. The *housekeeper* did it? (Did *what?*)

Chapter 9

In which "the boy" makes his first appearance and I make a bold move

Well, I've made it this far without mentioning "the boy," which must be some kind of a record for a seventh-grade girl. Sooner or later, I guess I have to introduce him. For now, let me just say that "the boy" is Rafael Arocho, and he is seriously *hot*. Raf (rhymes with "laugh") started out at St. Andrew's School, which is the boys' school right next door to St. Veronica's, but when his family moved across town at the end of sixth grade, he transferred to St. Thomas Aquinas, a boys' school on the Upper West Side. Rebecca and I have known him since kindergarten, and Margaret has known him since the third grade, when she moved to the city. Kids from the two schools were always being thrown together for assemblies, Christmas pageants, and other important events, so we got to know Raf and the other St. Andrew's boys pretty well. Up until fifth grade, we hated him; he was totally obnoxious, a typical boy. In the sixth grade, though, everything changed—he stopped acting like a *total* idiot and we started to appreciate some of his other qualities, if you know what I mean. And you do, right?

Here's how he enters the story: Margaret has just called to tell me she is on her way over when my phone rings again. It is Raf. After the usual complaining about how much homework the teachers are giving us, the subject changes to the upcoming dance at his school. The ones at St. Thomas Aquinas are rumored to be pretty entertaining.

"I'm going, but Margaret can't—her parents won't let her go to dances yet. Besides, she has Polish school on Saturday mornings, and she usually studies on Friday nights. I've got a couple of other friends, though, who are coming with me."

"Ah, Miss Sophie St. Popularity, never alone. Always draws a crowd."

"So, am I going to see *you* there? Or are you too cool for that sort of thing?"

"Well, yeah, of course I'm too cool for it. But I'll be there."

With that tantalizing nugget confirmed, I change the subject again. "Now, how are you at puzzles?"

"Like jigsaw puzzles?"

"More like word problems. Not crosswords, though. Remember those logic problems that Margaret used to torment us with?"

"Oh, yeah, those things. Like, Larry has three

brothers, Shemp is taller than Moe, but Moe is taller than Curly, so who's the tallest. That kind of thing?"

"Yep."

"Yeah, I'm actually pretty good at them. Why?"

"Meet me at Perkatory. Tomorrow, about four-thirty?"

"Wait. What's the big secret?"

"Just come. All will be revealed." And I hang up.

Hey, hold on a second. Did I just ask a boy out?

Chapter 10

In which Margaret reveals her human side

Since the clutter in my room is too much of a distraction for Margaret, I usually go to her apartment when we study together. (*Much* easier than cleaning.) It is a bit of a surprise, then, when she offers to come over that evening to study for a history test. I still have the phone in my hand when she plops down on my bed next to me.

"Who were you talking to?"

"Raf."

"Ohhhh."

"Whaddya mean, 'ohhhh'?"

"Nothing."

"Nothing? Just 'ohhhh?' "

"Yep." She smiles. "Just 'ohhhh.' "

"Ohhhh-kay. What's up with you? You hate studying here."

"I do not." She glances around the room at my books, some neatly stacked, others distinctly *not*. "All right, the, uh, disorder does trigger my OCD, but I have a solution." Sitting cross-legged on the floor, she closes her eyes and turns her palms upward, pretending to meditate. "Ohhmmmmm . . . Sophie's mess will not distract me . . . her ohmmmmess does not bother me . . . ohhhmmmmess . . ."

"We can go to your apartment," I say.

"Ooooommmmmmmmmmmmmmmmm—nope!"

I tackle her, pinning her shoulders to the bed. "Margaret Wrobel. What is going on with you?"

She tosses me off her. (For a skinny kid, she's freakishly strong.) "It's kind of nutty and crowded over there right now, with my grandmother, and my brother, and my parents. There's no privacy. It's more peaceful here."

"Right, I completely forgot about your grandmother. You haven't said anything since she got here. Is she sleeping in your room?"

Margaret's grandmother, eighty-four or eighty-five or eighty-six (no one seemed to know exactly), had recently arrived from Poland and was staying with them for a few weeks.

"Yeah."

"I thought she was your favorite. What did you call her?"

"My *babcia*. And she was my favorite. She *is*. I'm just . . ." Margaret rolls off the bed and starts to zip open her book bag. "Nothing. Forget it. Let's study. Where's your book?"

"Wait, for five years, all I've heard was Babcia this and Babcia that. About how *wonderful* and *amazing* she was, and about all the things you did together when you were back in Poland, and how much you missed her—and now she's here, and you haven't even introduced us yet."

Margaret looks miserable. "I know, I'm sorry. When my mom and dad told me she was coming, I was *so* happy. When I was a little kid, Babcia and I did *everything* together. She gave me my first violin and paid for my first lessons. I used to sit on her lap and fall asleep while she read to me. I remember riding the bus with her into Warsaw, singing our favorite song, and sometimes the other people on the bus would sing along with us. Almost all of my best memories from Poland are connected to her." She takes a deep breath and puts her head in her hands. "And now I just can't handle her."

"Why? What is she doing?"

"Well, for one thing, she talks *nonstop*. Since my grandfather died, she lives by herself in Poland, and I guess it's a treat having people to talk to. She goes to bed at seven-thirty, so I can't turn on the light or use my computer. And she keeps rearranging all my stuff! She says my skirt is too short and my shoes look like the ones the prostitutes in Warsaw wear—which is definitely *not* true. And every day, she tells my parents that I'll be ruined because I have a cell phone."

Hmmm. Doesn't sound *that* bad to me, but I want to

be supportive. "Maybe she's still settling in, you know, still getting over the jet lag, and once the novelty of having people around to talk to wears off, she'll be fine. Give her some time. In the meantime, we can hang here more often."

"Okay, but how about we straighten up those piles?"

"You mean you want to rearrange *my* stuff?"

I am whacked in the head with a pillow. Twice!

Chapter 11

In which a certain green-eyed character makes an appearance

During our review of the finer points of the French and Indian War, I clue Margaret in to my including Raf in our efforts to solve the puzzle. After all, if we can trust Leigh Ann, who we've known for like ten minutes, we ought to be able to trust an old friend like Raf, right? It takes a little convincing, but in the end she agrees that we aren't betraying Ms. Harriman. Having one more decent brain put to the task can't hurt. Never once do I let the fact that he seems to get better looking every time I see him or that I (kind of) miss having him around enter my decision-making process.

The next day, we walk into Perkatory a few minutes after four-thirty, and there he is, feet propped up on a scuzzy coffee table.

"Hey, losers. You're late." He flashes his gleaming white teeth at us.

We hug him anyway and squeeze in beside him on the couch.

"Where's Becca? I thought you three did everything together, like the Three Stooges."

"She had to stay home, but she knows what's going on," I assure him.

Leigh Ann walks in a few seconds later and takes a diet soda from the cooler. She catches a glimpse of us as she pays the cashier.

"Oh, hi, guys. What's up?" She smiles right at Rafael.

You should see the way they are looking at each other. And most unfortunately, Leigh Ann is kind of the female equivalent of Rafael. Face it, she's beautiful—the whole package. She's from the Dominican Republic and has this totally amazing skin and big brown eyes. Guys just go all stupid over her. She and Raf look like they just stepped out of a catalog.

Margaret, whose crush on Rafael is more theoretical and whose manners are *way* better than mine, introduces them. "Leigh Ann, meet our friend Raf. He used to go to St. Andrew's, but now he's over at Aquinas. Leigh Ann is new this year, but she's already part of the gang."

"Like Shemp," I say.

"Hi," says Leigh Ann.

"Hey," says Raf.

Genetically fortunate? Yes. Sparkling conversationalists? Not so much.

Boo-hoo, Leigh Ann can't stay! Alas, she has dance class and has to pirouette her way downtown. An awful shame. As soon as she leaves, I shove Raf on the shoulder. Hard.

"What's that for?"

I mimic the posture and smile he had affected for Leigh Ann. "Hey."

"What?" he says, totally pretending not to know what I am talking about.

"Could you be any more obvious?"

Margaret nods her assent. "She's right, Raf. You *were* kind of obvious." She leans forward and opens her backpack, ready for business. "But enough of this hormonal distraction."

Margaret and I tell him the whole story. If one of us leaves something out, the other jumps right in.

"Can I see this letter?" he asks.

Margaret hands him the copy.

Raf reads silently. "Jeez, who *was* this kid?"

"C'mon, you're *supposed* to be smart," I tease.

"*Margaret* is the smart one. *I'm* the good-looking one."

"Hey, what does that make me?"

"You—you're the—well—"

Is he blushing? Something strange is going on here. Another mystery?

"Focus!" says Margaret. "Does it make sense to you, as a puzzle? See, that's what I don't get. You have these two simple equations with six blanks, but only one clue. Find the answer and you get the next clue. But let's say we're able to figure out the clues. How does that help us solve the puzzle?"

"Yeah, shouldn't there be a map or something?" I say.

Raf hunches his shoulders. "Maybe one of the clues leads you to the map. So, what's in this for you guys, if you find it?"

"Well, nothing, really," Margaret says, "if you are referring to financial compensation."

"So you're doing this out of the kindness of your hearts?"

"*We're* doing this out of the kindness of *our* hearts," I correct. "You're going to help."

"Okay, okay, I'll do what I can. But I can't be coming over to this side of town every day. Crosstown buses are a nightmare."

Margaret shakes her head. "Oh, quit whining. You won't have to. This is a logic problem, and we're going to approach it logically—one step at a time, one clue at a time. No matter how smart this Caroline was, between the three of us and Rebecca and Leigh Ann, we should be able to solve it—*unless* . . ."

Wait a second—is that a crack in her relentless confidence?

"Unless what?"

"Well, what if one of the clues refers to something personal—something that only Caroline and her grandfather knew about?"

"Then we'll just have to ask Caroline," I say. "We know enough about her to track her down. But other than something like that, you guys do think we can solve it, right?"

Raf nods confidently. "Why not?"

Margaret snatches the letter back from Raf. "You see how he says that it's one of a pair, and that the other one is in the Met? We should go to the museum and look for the other one!" She is getting really excited again, her confidence firmly reasserted.

"Um, guys," Raf says. "Have you *been* to the Met? It could take you a week to find it there. Or it might be in storage someplace, or they could have sold it to another museum."

"Au contraire," I say. "We know exactly where to look. This guy, Caroline's grandfather, was an expert on early Christian relics, according to Ms. Harriman. That's where we'll go."

"Saturday?" Knowing that it is more command than question, both Raf and I agree to be on the steps of the museum at noon.

"Now, let's take a look at clue number one."

Time Management Margaret. We're together and we have a task to complete, so why put it off?

Chapter 12

In which I solve the first piece of the puzzle (and perhaps take more credit than I deserve–what's it to ya?)

The three of us put our brains together and figure out the first clue right there in Perkatory. Like *that*! I notice something about the letter from Caroline's grandfather that seems strangely coincidental. He said that he was certain that Caroline's knowledge of religion, classical languages, mathematics, literature, philosophy, and art should be sufficient to solve the puzzle. Six subjects, six clues. A coincidence? I think not. Were they listed in order? How the hell should I know? But it seems perfectly reasonable.

We settle on the idea that the clue refers to something in the field of religion and feel thoroughly confident. We *have* gone to Catholic schools all our lives, after all. Using a Magic Marker, Margaret prints the clue on a sheet of notebook paper and sets it on the table:

"It could be a sequence. You know, what comes next?" Raf suggests.

"Or a date," I say. "Isn't L used in Roman numerals?"

"L is fifty," Margaret answers. "But why mix types of numbers? What would it be, 502324? Doesn't make sense. L for 'left'? Left side of the church? Are the pews numbered, maybe?"

I scrunch up my face. "I don't think so. It kind of looks like a license plate number. Or a taxi number." I sound out the letters in my head but get nothing.

Raf sits up suddenly. "Oh my God. We need a Bible. It's a *religion* clue, remember? This is so easy."

Margaret immediately reaches into her bag.

"You have a copy of the Bible *with* you?" Raf shakes his head. "What are they doing to you at that school?"

"I have religion homework, you dope. Are you telling me you've never had one in your backpack? Wait—don't answer that. I don't even want to know how much homework you're *not* getting compared to us." She hands him a well-worn paperback.

"L is for Luke. L2324 is Luke 23:24," he says, flipping through the pages. "And before we go any further, the only reason I even thought of this is that we were just studying Luke the other day in class. Okay, here we go. Luke, chapter twenty-three, verse twenty-four: *And Pilate gave sentence that it should be as they required.*"

"Pontius Pilate sentencing Christ. The Crucifixion. Interesting." Margaret is deep in thought.

"*That's* the answer?" I ask.

"No, no, no—remember the letter. The clues lead us to places in the church. This is just telling us where to look!" Margaret checks her watch. "C'mon, get your stuff together; we're going over there right now, and we've got to move fast, because there's a Mass in about twenty minutes."

We scramble off to the imposing entrance to St. Veronica's Church. The slate-gray, late-afternoon sky is doing little to illuminate the church interior, and Father Danahey, the pastor, is apparently trying to save money on electricity, as the only lights on are those behind the altar. The rest of the church is eerily dark and nearly empty. A few people kneel in the pews, but no one even turns to look at us as we walk up the aisle on the right, pausing to show Raf the door with the stained glass chalice—the portal to the world of Ms. Harriman's past.

"What are we looking for this time?" I ask.

"Well, we know it's something to do with that verse about Pilate, something about the Crucifixion."

Raf takes a good look around. "There's like a thousand crucifixes in here."

"Shhh. Let me think." Margaret puts her hands over her ears to block out distractions and squints at the stone walls to our left and right. "The verse is very specific. If it were the verse where Jesus *dies* on the cross, *then* we would be looking for a crucifix. But our verse is about the *sentencing*. That's a totally different story. We're looking for Pontius Pilate."

"The paintings," I say, not altogether realizing that I have just hit the proverbial nail on the head. "Those 'station' things. Oh my God, I can't believe I know this. Remember, the other day when we were pretending to look at the one by the door, and, oh, what is that guy's name? The deacon. Mr., uh, Winter-butt-something."

"Winterbottom."

"That's it! Remember how he came by and talked to us about it? Well, remember the name of the artist—what he showed us on the back of the painting? It was *Harriman,* I'm sure of it. Mr. Winterbottom said that the painter's granddaughter lived next door, which must mean that Everett Harriman—the guy who wrote the note—was his son. C'mon, follow me. I'll show you."

I grab Raf by the arm and pull him, with Margaret following, to the first station and point at the brass plaque attached to the bottom of the frame. "Look at the title. I noticed it the other day while you were playing around with the lock."

Margaret bends over and in the dim light reads,

"*Jesus Is Condemned to Death*. Sophie, you're a genius!"

I feel so incredibly proud, even if I'm still not sure what exactly I have done.

"Let's look at the back of the painting, or maybe the wall behind it." Margaret checks to see if the coast is clear. She runs her fingers around the edge of the gaudy gold frame and then lifts one edge of the painting away from the wall and peers at the back side of the frame and canvas.

"It's too dark. You wouldn't happen to have a flashlight on you, would you?"

Raf reaches into his pocket. "How about a lighter?"

"That'll work," said Margaret. "Give it here."

"Are you crazy?" I immediately have this vision of the painting catching fire. There has to be a special place in hell for people who burn religious paintings—even mediocre ones. "And hey, how come you have a lighter, anyway?" I hiss at Raf. "Are you smoking again?" When we were in the sixth grade, Raf stole a pack of cigarettes from his uncle and went through this "I am cool, therefore I smoke" phase. His mom found out and told him that if she so much as ever *smelled* a cigarette in his vicinity, she would kill him more painfully than the cancer ever would.

Margaret has her entire head behind the painting, moving from one side to the other. "Hey, I think I found something. Raf, do you have a knife?"

I think I might just explode. "What! A *knife*? Oh my God."

"Oh, relax, Soph. I just need to pry something out. There's a thumbtack stuck into the wood in the back, and it looks like it's attached to something."

"How about a nice, nonlethal nail file?" I suggest.

"That'll work."

I hand it to her and she disappears behind the painting again.

"Got it!" She comes out holding a folded piece of yellowed paper, about one inch square, with a red thumbtack stuck through the center of it. "Let's take it out where there's better light. There's something written on it, but it's really tiny."

Almost on cue, more lights come on in the church as preparations are made for the five-thirty Mass. As a group, we move directly beneath a light fixture, and Margaret holds out her palm so we are all able to read the paper as she unfolds it.

Congratulations! You have found the first answer.

$(i) = x$

The clue for (ii) is on the back. Good luck!

On the back, the lettering is in the opposite direction. It looks like this:

S
IE
AR
IS
OV
LE
RB
MA
HE
RT
DE
UN
OK
LO

Oh, come on. I mean, the first clue is X? Who but a math teacher would make that an *answer*? Don't get me wrong, after English, math is probably my next favorite subject. I absolutely hate all those otherwise intelligent kids who insist that they're just no good at math, when the reason they're no good at math is that they sleep in class and then don't do the homework and—surprise!— they don't understand it and, gee, I wonder why they're having trouble. And yes, I know that is a run-on sentence, but I am trying to make a point.

"You know, when you think about it, the X has an

important place in the history of the treasure hunt," Raf says. "X *always* marks the spot, right?" He checks his watch. "Hey, it's been great, but I gotta run. So, see you Saturday, ya losers?"

"Saturday, dear butthead," Margaret says. "At noon, on the Met steps."

As we turn for the back of the church, I catch a glimpse of a man exiting through the heavy carved wooden doors. I looked around the church just a few seconds earlier, and I swear he wasn't there. The hair on the back of my neck stands up—a terrible and ominous sign.

Chapter 13

In which the astounding shallowness of my character is revealed

Rebecca calls me at home that night to hear about the meeting of the minds at Perkatory and to share her doubts about the whole thing.

"But it's not just that the *ring* might be gone. It would take a miracle for all six clues to still be there."

"True. But finding that thumbtack comes pretty close to proving that nobody else knew about the 'buried treasure.'"

"Have you figured out what the deal is with the two equations? I don't get how filling in the blanks in those two problems is going to lead you to the treasure."

"No idea. Margaret and Raf think that when we *need* to know, we will. Until then—"

"And speaking of your *friend* Rafael, how is he?"

"What do you mean?" I say defensively. "He *is* just a friend."

"Uh-huh. Sure. Well, *if* that's true—tell me again,

why is that true? Jeez, Sophie, he is like, better looking every time I see him."

Et tu, Rebecca?

"Yeah, well, apparently you're not the only one who thinks so. You should have seen Leigh Ann flirting with him."

"Leigh Ann? Oh, God. When did *she* meet him?" The way she says it freaks me out even more than I already am.

"When we were in Perkatory. She comes in, and she is all flipping her hair and being her stunning self—well, you know how she is. And Raf was just as bad. I wanted to kill him. I don't want to think about it. So, about the dance Friday, at Aquinas? You *are* still going to that, aren't you?"

"Um . . ."

"Oh, come on, Rebecca. Margaret's not allowed to go, so if you don't go, it's just going to be me and Bridget. Pleeeez don't do that to me. You *have* to go."

Bridget O'Malley is a notoriously boy-crazy friend. We were really close in elementary school, but over the last couple of years, her top priority has definitely shifted from school to boys, and frankly, she's kind of scary to be around.

"C'mon. Lots of people you know are going."

"Nobody that I really care about, though. Won't your mom let you go?"

"Actually, she said I should go, but I still know she's really not happy about it."

"Yeah, well, my dad still thinks I'm ten years old. He *actually* asked me if I was going to wear my uniform— to the dance!"

"Sophie, I was thinking I should offer to babysit so Mom can go out and see a movie or something. Her friend Alice called here a little while ago and said something about it, but I know Mom, and she'll say no so I can go to the dance instead."

"So? Go to the dance," I say, completely glossing over the generous thing that my friend is offering to do.

"But that's not fair. She needs the movie and the time with her friend a lot more than I need to go to a stupid dance."

Slowly—at the speed of your average slug—I start to understand and appreciate the sacrifice that Rebecca is willing to make.

"Ohhhhhhh. Man, you are a good kid. You're so *nice.* Now I feel bad for pushing you. Hey, how about I come over and hang with you?"

"Sophie St. Pierre, you have to go to that stupid dance. *Somebody* has to tell me what happens at these stupid things! And besides, what about stupid Rafael? Isn't he going?"

Damn. Yes, he is going, and yes, he'll be incredibly pissed if all three of us don't show, but I find myself saying out loud: "So? He'll get over it. I'm sure Leigh Ann will be there to fill in for me."

Oy. That last part hurts.

"But my brother and sister will be here, and they'll

want to watch *Balto* for like the millionth time. And I don't even have a decent Internet connection anymore. We're back to dial-up."

"I don't care. My parents were gonna give me money for the dance, so I'll have enough for pizza. And I'll stop by my dad's restaurant after school tomorrow and pick up some desserts. They're awesome, I promise."

"You're serious."

"In fact, I will seriously call Margaret and tell her she's coming, too. We'll have a little party. She can bring her books with her if she wants, and maybe we can work on the skit for the Dickens banquet. Are you okay with this? I mean, I guess I kind of invited myself over."

"It's very cool," Rebecca says. "Bring dessert. And, Soph?"

"What?"

"Thanks."

"Duh. You would do the same thing for me."

"Eh. Maybe."

"Maybe?"

"Well, definitely not if Raf was waiting for *me*."

"Jerk."

"Loser."

"Just for that, you are *not* getting out of this Dickens thing."

"G'night, Soph."

Chapter 14

In which Wile E. Coyote and Balto fight to the death. Well, not really, but wouldn't that be cool?

On Friday night, while everyone who is someone (at least at St. V's) is headed for the West Side and a night of dancing and who knows what else (will I *ever* know?), Margaret and I take the subway down to Canal Street and do a little shopping before heading over to Rebecca's apartment. You can find just about anything you need, and a lot of things no one in their right mind would ever want, on Canal Street. In its own way, it is a fabulous budget-shopping experience. Designer knockoff handbags? Check. Cute little Chinese ballet shoes? Got 'em, any color you want for a buck! Jangly, dangly earrings? Right here, miss—two for five dollars. We resist the urge to buy illegal movies that are still playing in the theaters, but I do pick up a beat-up-looking disc with a bunch of cartoons for Rebecca's little sibs and, well, a really cute belt and a pair of big sunglasses that I just *can't* resist.

Margaret had agreed to go with me to Rebecca's, provided that I left her alone after school from four to seven so she could catch up on her studying. Her grandmother and parents went to Queens to visit some relatives, so she had three hours of serious "quiet time." I was forbidden to contact her or bother her in any way. In addition to my temporary exile from Margaretland, Rafael is miffed at me for bailing on the dance. But the first thing he did after I told him that we weren't going was ask whether my friend Leigh Ann would be there. AAAAAAGGGGHHHHH! Is this the cost of "doing the right thing?" I may not be cut out for it.

My dad, on the other hand, came through with a box full of miniature chocolate tortes, Napoleons, éclairs, *and* truffles. I may have lost the boy (temporarily), but I have the primo goodies.

At Becca's we order pizza, and after it comes, as Rebecca predicted, her little sibs clamor to watch *Balto* yet again.

"No! I can't listen to that damn thing one more time," she says.

"You said a swear. I'm telling," says her little brother, Jonathan.

"You're damn right I did, mini-man. No more *Balto*. Look, here are some cartoons that my nice friend brought just for you. There's Bugs Bunny and the Road Runner. These are *classics*. I guarantee you're gonna love them."

Jonathan and his twin sister, Jennifer, whine, but

after thirty seconds of the Road Runner's "beep-beeps," they are enraptured. (I just finished the "Word Power" in an old *Reader's Digest* in my orthodontist's office. I am *enraptured* by the word "enraptured.") The disc also turns out to be a serendipitous choice (more "Word Power"). How could I have known that the Road Runner and his arch-nemesis Wile E. Coyote would help us with clue number two?

"Okay, here it is," Margaret says, printing the letters on a sheet of newsprint torn from Rebecca's sketchpad.

S
IE
AR
IS
OV
LE
RB
MA
HE
RT
DE
UN
OK
LO

We all stare at it for a long, long time, nobody saying anything.

"Is this the classical languages clue?" I ask. "Because I have to tell you: I've got nothin'."

Margaret and Rebecca both look hypnotized—that's how hard they are concentrating.

"Is it a code?" Rebecca asks.

"Maybe. But for now, let's look for easier solutions," Margaret suggests. "What if it's a list of words, and he's only showing us two letters from each one?"

"But there could be *thousands* of possible words for some of those," Rebecca says.

"Yeah, you're right. Is it, say, a famous quote? Or another Bible verse? That would narrow it down."

Rebecca seems skeptical. "I don't know. That seems *too* hard. Maybe if there were blanks to fill in the missing letters. That way, at least you'd know how many letters were missing. Do me a favor and write the letters out the usual way, across the page."

SIEARISOVLERBMAHERTDEVNOKLO

"I think that made it worse," I say.

"Are there *any* recognizable words in there?" asks Margaret. "Anything longer than two letters? What about every other letter? S, E, R, S, V, E—no, that doesn't work. Damn. Reverse? O, K, N, E, T. Nope."

"Hey, wait a minute," Rebecca says. "Let me see the letter. What was the first clue? The exact wording?"

" 'Look behind L2324.' Why?"

Rebecca's brow furrows and she scratches her

head, thinking hard, eyes darting back and forth across the paper, and then, finally, a satisfied smile appears on her face. "*Look behind*—all right! I'm definitely onto something. Look at this. Take the last two pairs of letters."

OK
LO

"OK and LO, right? Now, move the LO up one row, in front of the OK. What do you have? LOOK, right? Now, do the same thing with the next letters." She writes:

UN DE

LO OK

"Now, just keep sliding the ones from the bottom of the list up and in front of the next ones up." She continues on the paper:

UN DE RT HE
UNDER THE
And finally,
LOOK UNDER THE
"Damn, Rebecca," I say, in awe.
"I'm with Sophie," said Margaret.

Now that we (as if I had anything to do with it!) have the pattern, the rest is a snap. We end up with this:

LOOK UNDER THE MARBLE OVISARIES

But OVISARIES means nothing to us.

"Sounds kinda like 'ovaries,' " I note.

Margaret chuckles. "I don't think Caroline's grandfather would tell her to look under *those*. Which leaves us two possibilities. One, OVISARIES is an anagram—"

"Another one?" says Rebecca.

"Or this one definitely is the classical languages clue and OVISARIES is Greek or Latin. You don't happen to have a Latin dictionary around, do you?"

"Yeah, I've got one in the kitchen," Rebecca says. "I think it's in the freezer."

"Margaret thinks everyone has a full reference library in their house," I assure her.

"In *her* house," Margaret corrects. " 'Everyone' is a singular pronoun."

"Let's just kill her now," I say. "No one will know, but even if they did, they'd never blame us."

"Well, how about a regular English dictionary, then."

"*That* I have." Rebecca goes into her room to fetch a perfectly ordinary, respectable paperback dictionary. Margaret's personal dictionary is six inches thick and outweighs her by a good twenty pounds.

While the gears in Margaret's brain whir and click like something out of a cartoon, I head into the other room to watch the real thing with the kids. Rebecca's brother and sister don't even look up when I enter the room; they are *deeply* involved. I sit on the floor next to them.

Suddenly Margaret starts shouting out all this stuff about how while she was searching for "ovisaries" in the dictionary, she found the word "ovine," which means "of, or having the nature of, a sheep," from the Latin *ovis,* for "sheep."

After sort of half listening for a while, I say, in an off-hand kind of way, "Oh, it's probably like *Road-runnerus digestus* or *Carnivorous vulgaris.*"

"Sophie, what *are* you babbling about? Get back in here," Margaret orders.

"I was *babbling* that it's probably the scientific name for an animal, like *Road-runnerus digestus* or *Carnivorous vulgaris.* You know, how in the Road Runner cartoons, about once an episode, they do this thing where the stupid coyote is chasing the dumb bird, and they'll freeze the frame, so it looks like something out of a biology textbook. And at the bottom of the page, they come up with these crazy fake Latin names—well, I assume they're fake, anyway—like, for the coyote, *Road-runnerus digestus.*"

"The genus and the species," says Margaret. "Of course! *Ovis aries* is the Latin name of some kind of sheep!"

"So I'm right? Again?"

Margaret beams at me and immediately runs to Rebecca's computer, and within, well, minutes—using

Rebecca's dial-up Internet, no less—we know that *Ovis aries* is, in fact, the Latin name for the common domestic sheep. Somewhere in the church, we hope, is a marble sheep we can look under. But not at its ovaries.

Just one more thought about the Road Runner: if that stupid coyote can afford all that stuff from the Acme Corporation, why doesn't he just buy something to eat? Am I right? You know I am.

Chapter 15

In which Margaret discovers
my dirty little secret

If we didn't *know* that the church was locked, we probably would be packing up the kids and taking the subway uptown to Sixty-eighth Street to find whatever it is that awaits us under the sheep. But since we can't do that, and since I just *have* to tell someone, I have a, um, perfectly valid reason to call Raf. Because, you know, he's my friend. What is going on with me?

Life in elementary school had been pretty simple; St. V's was like my all-girls galaxy, with St. Andrew's—the boys' galaxy—right next door. Both are smallish galaxies with enough contact between them that I knew just about everyone in my grade in both schools. The St. Andrew's boys may not have been anything spectacular, but they were *our* boys. Now that we are in the upper school, suddenly they are *everybody's* boys. People like Leigh Ann, who can't possibly appreciate Raf the way I can, have a chance. More than a chance, actually, because to Raf she is new and different and exciting—not just his good ol' punch-each-other-on-the-arm pal.

So I call him. And Leigh Ann is right there, with him—well, *near* him at least. Raf even puts her on the phone to talk to me. *Sheesh!* Utterly clueless.

On the way home from Rebecca's, Margaret asks me about the phone call. "What happened? One second you're happy, you're talking to Raf, and the next second, poof, you're moping around like your dog ran away. Did you tell him how we figured out the second clue?"

"I tried, but it was hard to hear with the music and everything."

"So what else is the problem?"

"Guess."

"What? I have no idea. What is going on?"

"Oh, it's nothing," I lie. "It's just—he was there with Leigh Ann. And I think I'm losing my mind."

"Oh."

"Exactly."

"Sophie, do you *like* Raf?"

To paraphrase my grandmother, I hem and haw. "I don't. I mean, I don't know. This is so embarrassing. I *can't* like him. Oh, God, why am I like this?"

"What exactly *are* you 'like'?"

"Like an idiot girl who is freaking out because he put *her* on the phone."

"He did? That's weird."

"Tell me about it. She's like, 'Why aren't you guys

here? I miss you. It's not the same without you, blah, blah, blah.' And that's the thing that drives me the craziest. Part of me wants to hate her, but I really don't think she was rubbing my face in it or anything. She actually sounded like she wished we were there."

"So you *want* to hate her, but you don't have a good reason, because she really is as nice as she seems. Is that about right?"

"Pretty much," I admit.

"Soph, they just met. You don't even know if anything is—"

"Oh, come on. You saw them at the coffee shop. The way they looked at each other. They are *so* going to hook up."

Margaret puts her arm around me. "I'm sorry. I'm still a little surprised, but I'm sorry. You might have mentioned this. This is Margaret; remember me? And I don't think you're crazy. But don't jump to any conclusions—yet. Give it a little time. Okay?"

"Yeah. I do feel better just talking about it a little. This way, I can hear how loony I sound."

"You're not loony. It's just love—"

"Or something like it."

Chapter 16

In which I learn what stuff dreams are made of on a Saturday morning at the Metropolitan Museum of Art

Undoubtedly because she feels sorry for pathetic little me, Margaret agrees to put off going to the church to look under the sheep until after we are finished at the museum. (That sentence must sound totally bizarre to someone who just randomly opened up to this page to see what this story is all about. Go back and start at the beginning!) Rebecca calls me in the morning to say that she, too, will meet us.

I act incredibly normal when I see Raf, teasing him about how bad his hair looks and questioning whether his shirt should even be on the same block as his pants. (They *shouldn't*.) What *is* truly remarkable, though, about his appearance on the steps of the museum is that he is on time for the second time inside of a week. He was *always* late for everything when he was at St. Andrew's.

104

"So, are we goin' in? And, uh, weren't you supposed to bring coffee?"

"After we find what we're looking for, then we'll stop for coffee," says Margaret. "But you can't take too long, because we've got to go to the church to look for our *Ovis aries.*"

"You know, that reminds me of something I was gonna mention last night," I say. "I don't think they're going to let us wander around the church looking under statues and paintings whenever we feel like it. Priests and nuns and security guards—even when they're half blind and deaf like that Robert guy—tend to be a little touchy about stuff like that."

"Yeah, they're gonna think we're planning a heist or something," Raf adds.

"Oh, don't you worry your pretty little head about that," Margaret says, further mussing up his mussy hair. "I've got a plan."

Like Joan of Arc leading the troops to battle, Margaret of Manhattan leads us straight through the museum's main lobby (the "Great Hall") and then into the Medieval Art wing, where dump-truck loads of the treasures of the churches of Europe are displayed on the walls and in glass cases scattered around the various rooms. "Okay, it *should* be around here somewhere." Taking me by the arm, she guides me to a section of stained glass window from the Cathedral of Saint-Pierre in France. A good omen?

She unfolds the paper that contains all the information we have so far. "Remember, we're looking for stuff donated by this Zoltan guy, especially something that could be one of a pair."

Zoltan. Sounds like the name of a god, or at least someone with superpowers. Hmm . . . Zoltan St. Pierre.

"Like a pair of earrings?" Rebecca wonders.

"Maybe," says Margaret. "But he probably wouldn't give her one earring, so I'm guessing it's a ring with some kind of Christian symbol on it."

We barely start looking when—*ta-da!*—Margaret hones in on a beautiful gold ring centered in a display case in a place of honor above the lesser pieces. It is set with a cross of tiny rubies. The plaque sitting next to it informs us that the ring had been found in the ruins of a twelfth-century chapel near Rocamadour, France, and donated to the museum by the estate of one Zoltan Ressanyi, the Hungarian-American archaeologist and explorer. It is "the groom's ring from a pair of wedding rings known as the Rings of Rocamadour." According to local legend, the rings had been a gift to a young couple from St. Veronica, who had touched them to the famous veil—the one she wiped the face of Christ with. They had been passed down through the centuries, and those who wear the rings, it is said, are visited in their dreams by St. Veronica, who answers their prayers.

"Holy crap," I say. "That's what we're looking for? It's beautiful. Oh my God. How much is something like that worth?"

"It is, in fact, priceless," says a man's voice.

We all spin around in shock. And there he is—Mr. Malcolm Chance, decked out in layers and layers of tweed and still carrying that ridiculous walking stick.

Aha! I *had* seen someone sneak out of the church. That jerk must have been snooping and heard our plans. The hair on the back of my neck stands up again as I catch another whiff of his strange odor. What *is* that smell?

"Of course, it would be worth even more if it were reunited with its companion. There's no telling what the museum might pay to have the two Rings of Rocamadour reunited."

Margaret totally keeps her cool. "Dr. Chance, right? We met you at Ms. Harriman's the other day."

But old Malcolm plays it pretty cool, too, as if our running into each other in the museum is just a coincidence. "Oh, yes, of course. How do you do? Are you students interested in early Christian artifacts? Or just this one in particular?"

"We're doing a little research project for school," I fib. "It's more like one of those treasure hunts where teachers send you out with a list of things to find." I glance quickly at the others to make sure they are with me.

"My, my. That sounds interesting. I'm afraid my education was a bit less, shall we say, creative. Lots of memorizing and reciting, I seem to recall. Is there anything else—for your little *project*—that I can help you find? I'm something of an expert in this field," he says, gesturing to encompass everything in the room.

I *so* want to kick him in the shins.

Margaret sensibly chooses a more mature response. "No, thank you. I think we're all set. We just need to copy down some information."

Malcolm leans over the case. "This ring you're so interested in—the Ring of Rocamadour—quite a thing of rare beauty, no?"

"The stuff that dreams are made of," says Raf, quoting his favorite Sam Spade line from *The Maltese Falcon*. (Every time he says it, Margaret points out that the line was ripped off from Shakespeare.) Raf's grandfather was a projectionist at a theater in Times Square in the forties and fifties, and he and Raf spend hours and hours watching old movies (and yes, I know, lots of great movies are in black and white, and I should give them a chance instead of watching *Grease* for the six hundredth time). A lot of the big premieres took place in Times Square in those olden days, and Raf's grandfather has a million stories about all the movie stars who had been to *his* theater.

"My, my, a young Dashiell Hammett fan. Or is it Shakespeare? Either way, a great line, isn't it?" Malcolm looks at the three of us and takes a deep breath. "It is apparent that the four of you are quite intelligent, so there's no point in my beating about the bush. I know why you're here and what you're really looking for. I have not yet ascertained exactly *how* you came to be looking for it, but that's not particularly important right now. What is important is that this—this object you seek—*is* found, and found soon. You are probably *not* aware that the church is about to undergo a thorough cleaning and sprucing up, from the tiles of the floor to the limestone blocks of that spectacular vaulted ceiling.

"And do not forget that I *knew* Everett Harriman quite well, too. I was, in many respects—regardless of what my former wife may have told you—his protégé. I also knew of his intention to provide my daughter with the puzzle you seem to have stumbled on. And perhaps more than anyone else, I know how his mind worked. Judging from what I've seen and heard thus far, some of what you need may be in danger of disappearing very soon. So, then, shouldn't we join forces to prevent that from occurring?"

I stand up straight and look him directly in the eyes. "Look, Mr. Chance, we're doing a project for our religion class, and we already found what we were looking for. We are *not* a force, and we *won't* be joining you."

He stares right back at me, half smiling and half smirking. Smirkling? "It's strange, don't you think, a teacher asking you to remove something from the back of a painting? Risking damage to one of the church's treasures, for the sake of this 'project.' "

"We didn't damage anything."

"Perhaps."

"Are you spying on us?" I blurt out. "This is no co-incidence—you just happening to be here at the same time as us."

"Easy, Soph." Margaret pulls me back a step. "Dr. Chance, even if everything you say is true, how can we be sure we can trust you?"

"A fair question. Let me answer it with another. Why should you *not* trust me?" He waves his hand around the room. "This has been my career, my life. I'm not the monster I fear Elizabeth makes me out to be. You don't have to give me your answer right now. Think about it— but not for too long."

And with that, Malcolm smiles, tips his cap to us, and walks his tweedy, creepy, strange-smelling self away. Ick, ick, ick.

Chapter 17

In which our "school project" seems to be taking on a life of its own

After we watch him stroll down the length of the gallery and out the door, Rebecca speaks up. "Man, that guy gives me the creeps. How he snuck up on us like that— oh my God. I almost peed my pants. And what is up with that stick? He doesn't even need it. And did you notice that smell?"

"Yes, yes, and yes!" I say. "I can't figure it out. It's right on the tip of my brain—"

"It's hair dye," Margaret says. "That stuff men use when their hair turns gray. My dad uses it. Come on, do you really think he's *that* bad? I think he's kind of, um, charming."

I pretend to gag. "Oh, come on, Margaret. How can you *not* see it? The guy is pure evil."

That makes her laugh out loud. "Sophie, he's just an old man."

"We'll see," I mutter, slightly miffed.

"How much do you think he knows?" Raf asks as we cross Fifth Avenue on our way down to the church. We are rushing and all of us keep looking over our shoulders for any sign of the "old dude with the stick," as Raf calls him.

"I think he's mostly fishing," I say. "He overheard part of what we said in the church and when I opened my big fat mouth at Ms. Harriman's."

"He knows about the ring," Margaret points out. "And that it's hidden somewhere, probably in the church. But obviously, without the letter, none of that matters. I *am* worried about what he said about the renovation work in the church. That could be a problem. So—let's go to church!"

A short subway ride later, we are in front of the church, watching a giddy bride and groom bounding down the steps and into a stretch SUV. Adoring family members and friends pelt them with birdseed as a flock of pigeons pace nearby, waiting for their chance to celebrate the blessed event.

"Poor guy," says Raf, watching the smiling groom pull the door of the limousine shut.

Margaret smiles slyly. "That'll be you one day, Raf. And who knows? Maybe even to someone we know." She pokes a finger into my ribs.

Rebecca sees that. "Is there something going on I don't know about?"

"No!" I say, hurrying everyone along.

Raf, of course, is oblivious. "Hey, can we get a slice or something? I'm starving."

"Oh, you can wait a little while," Margaret says. "We won't be that long."

We're standing at the foot of the steps when Rebecca says, "Guys, I'm gonna take off now. I'm meeting with Ms. Harriman at that gallery in Chelsea. Call me later and tell me what you found."

Margaret and I hug her as if she is moving to some remote corner of the planet.

"Good luck!"

"Call us! Do you have your sketchbook?"

"Say hi to Elizabeth!"

"You're going to be famous!"

Rebecca stops us. "Guys, I'm just going to *talk* to this woman. It's no big deal. I promise I'll call you later."

When she leaves, Margaret, Raf, and I race up the church steps (I win!) and find ourselves face to face with our good friend Robert, who peeks at us over his *Glamour* magazine and sighs.

"Hi! Remember me? Margaret Wrobel, from St. Veronica's? Here's my ID. I was wondering if it would be okay if we took some pictures of the stained glass behind the altar."

Robert looks up at her with a mixture of confusion, suspicion, and annoyance. Apparently, without our blazers, we don't look so innocent.

"WE PROMISE NOT TO TOUCH ANYTHING. IT'S FOR A VERY SPECIAL SCHOOL PROJECT."

"WHY ARE YOU SHOUTING?" he shouts, adjusting his hearing aid. "You should probably check with Mr. Winterbottom. He's around somewhere. There's another wedding at four-thirty, so he'll be supervising while they set up flowers and so forth."

"Oh, okay. No problem. We know him. He's the one who helped us out the other day. Thanks!" That Margaret. So sincere, so cheerful. How can anyone *not* trust her? We have now used that lame "school project" excuse three times. It's like my dad says: if it's not broken, don't fix it.

Mr. Winterbottom, pant cuffs dragging and shoulders drooping, is at the front of the church muttering to himself. When he sees us approaching, he squints hard and forces a smile. "Good afternoon, girls—and boy. Here on a Saturday! It seems you just can't bear to stay away from church."

Dutiful smiles all around.

"Mr. Winterbottom, we'd like to take a few pictures," Margaret says. "Do you think it would be all right if we go back by those windows behind the altar? They're nice and low, so I can get really close."

"Sure, just be careful not to knock anything over." His smile reveals a set of teeth just crying out for a bleaching. "Something in particular I can help you find?"

Margaret assures him that she has it under control

and leads the way, genuflecting before stepping onto the raised marble floor. Raf and I, good Catholic kids that we are, follow her example and then start looking for our *Ovis aries*. Plenty of sheep in the area behind the altar, all right—painted sheep, stained glass sheep, embroidered sheep, but nothing made of marble. I'm looking at one of the windows when I spot Mr. Winterbottom. For somebody who *seems* like he trusts us, he sure is keeping a close eye on our little trio. We start moving around the perimeter of the church, checking all the little chapels and niches built into the stone walls, each containing a sculpture or two. St. Francis, as usual, is surrounded by several animals—but no sheep. We search our way around the church, with Mr. Winterbottom never more than a stone's throw away—and my throwing arm is not that great.

Margaret doesn't seem concerned, about either the shortage of marble sheep or Mr. Winterbottom's close proximity. "Remember, there's more to the church than just this part. For instance, the passages that led us to Ms. Harriman's. Plus, there's the outside of the building. The note says 'in or on' the church."

And then I swear I see an actual lightbulb light up over Margaret's head. A hundred watts, at least.

"Soph, do you have the copy of the note? Let me see it for a sec."

I dig through my bag. "Here you go, Miss Marple." (Hey, I read, too.)

Scanning the note, Margaret smiles.

"You've got a scary look in your eyes," Raf says.

"Where's Mr. Winterbottom? We need him!"

Raf and I stare open-mouthed as Margaret bounds down the aisle toward Mr. Winterbottom, who is pretending to refill the holy-water urns in the back of the church.

"Um, Mr. Winterbottom, I'm sorry to bother you again, but I have a little question. Kind of a strange question, actually. When does the official Christmas stuff—you know, the Nativity set and all that—when do you bring all that stuff out?"

"The *Official* Christmas Stuff?" A genuine smile. "Right after Thanksgiving, the start of the Advent season. Not for a few weeks. May I ask why?"

For a second, Margaret looks stumped. "Well, it's kind of a long story, but it's related to that project we told you about. Sort of. I want to look at the bottoms, to see where they were made. Do you know, by any chance, where they're all stored?"

"Of course. I know exactly where *everything* in the church is."

"It would be great if we could see it—just for a minute. I mean, if it's not too much trouble."

"For this rather exciting and unusual school project, right?" He looks skeptical but is still smiling—as though he is willing to have one put over on him.

"I promise it will only take a few seconds," says

Margaret. "I—we only need to see one of them to take a look at the markings."

"Well, all right. I have a few minutes before people start showing up for this wedding; I guess I can show you the storage room."

A few moments later, he leads us through the door with the stained glass chalice. Margaret and I grin knowingly at each other as he digs into his pockets for the skeleton key that unlocks it. Rebecca did it faster with a bobby pin.

"Right in here," he says, continuing to lead the way. "There's a storage closet down the hall. I was in here just the other day, looking for—well, for something I had, uh, misplaced."

Raf whispers in my ear. "Breath mints? A suit that actually fits?"

I know it's really mean, but I have to bite my finger to keep from laughing.

He opens the closet door and fumbles around for the light switch, finally finding it. "I never remember where that darn switch is."

Turns out it's a pretty funny sight that greets us. The Nativity scene is set up, but all the pieces are crammed together facing the door. The statues of Joseph and Mary, along with the shepherds, the angels, and the three wise men, look as if they can't wait to be set free from the tight confines of their off-season prison.

"Can I touch them?" Margaret asks.

"Oh, sure. Just be careful, especially with the infant Jesus. His arms have been broken off a number of times, from the looks of things. They're quite old, you know. Worth more than you might think."

As I take a closer look, I see that both arms have been glued back onto the body. Margaret shoots me a look and I ask Mr. Winterbottom about the passageway we've just come through; where did it lead, who used it, and so on. Lucky for me, he *loves* talking about the church, and before I know it, he's telling me to duck and we're going up the stairs that lead to Ms. Harriman's door. He points out all the architectural details and statues of the saints set into the niches along the walls, and I pretend to be just *fascinated* by it all, even asking him about a striking little statue of St. Andrew. By the time we get back to the storage closet, Margaret and Raf are waiting for us, grinning like idiots—thanks to my masterful diversion of poor, sweet Mr. Winterbottom.

We thank him profusely and practically run out the side door of the church. As soon as we get outside, Raf and I crowd around Margaret. But we also check to see if anyone is watching or listening.

"So, where was it? Have you read it yet? What does it say?"

"It was under a little lamb lying right next to the manger," Margaret answers. "His legs are folded underneath his body, and there's a crevice where *this* was stuck in." She hands me a tiny scroll, tied with a piece of black thread. "You do the honors."

I unroll the paper.

Congratulations again! You are well on your way!

(ii) = 3Y

The clues for (iii) and (iv) are on the back.

Then I turn it over to reveal:

(iii) = 612 ÷ D

D = the Distance (rounded to the nearest whole foot) between the centers of the south and west rose windows.

The answer to this clue is simply a number; therefore I am also providing the clue for (iv):

One of the following characters doesn't belong in this list:

Drummle, Guppy, Heep, Steerforth, Traddles, Pirrip, Summerson, Squeers, Copperfield, Scrooge

That character's first name is the same as the last name of someone who donated a single church pew. Look behind the brass plaque that bears that name.

"So, 3Y goes in the second blank," Margaret says. "Now we have X + 3Y = something. And *two* more clues."

Raf scratches his head. "Maybe this whole thing is like a video game, where there are lots of levels, and we're still in the first one."

I suggest that we ask for help, but Margaret wants nothing to do with that idea. "No way. Jeez, we just started and we've already got two of the clues figured out. And now we're getting a handle on how his mind works—er, worked."

"I'm still not sure how we got this one. I mean, how did you know to ask about the Christmas stuff?"

"Because I *observed,* Dr. Watson," Margaret says. "It was simple, really. Look at the date on the letter to Caroline. December ninth. As soon as I remembered that, I realized that when he wrote the letter, the Nativity set would have been displayed on the altar. It was obvious."

"To *you.*"

"Let's get some obvious pizza," says Raf. "I'm *obviously* starving."

Margaret hands me some money. "Why don't you guys pick up some slices at Ray's and take them over to Perkatory. I'll meet you there in a few minutes." Her hands go over her ears, the sure sign that she is deep in thought.

"What are *you* going to do?"

"I want to take a look at one more thing inside. I'll tell you about it later. It's only going to take me a few minutes, I promise."

She turns and runs back up the steps while Raf drags me down the street to Famous Ray's Pizza. (Or is it Original Ray's? Or Famous Original Ray's? I can never remember.)

Chapter 18

This one is for all the people who say they've never used geometry in real life

Despite the way it sounds, wandering around the Metropolitan Museum of Art and St. Veronica's Church and then sitting down to some serious puzzle-solving in the coffee shop with Raf is *not* a bad way to spend a Saturday. And Margaret, of course. There are these two old booths in the back corner at Perkatory, and when Raf and I show up with the pizza, she practically shoves me into the seat next to him, her eyes sparkling mischievously as she tries (totally unsuccessfully) to suppress a knowing smile. It's a small booth, so it is practically impossible to sit without touching each other. Boy oh boy. This boy.

And so, I eat my slice, drink my Dr. Brown's cream soda, and listen to Raf's stories from the dance the night before. (No mention of *her*—is he hiding something?) Apparently, things got a little out of hand on the dance floor. Now, let me say right here that I am not a prude; I mean, my dad is French, for God's sake; we've had some pretty frank discussions around the dinner table. Margaret just about died of embarrassment one time when she was over for dinner once and my parents started talking about their "first times."

"Yeah, you can't believe some of the moves kids were doing," Raf says. "Here, let me show you." He pulls me out of the booth and spins me around so that my back is to his front. His hands are resting on my hips. "Okay, now—"

"Stop it!" I snap, spinning away from him. My fingers and toes start to tingle as every last drop of blood in my body rushes to my face.

"Why, Sophie, my dear, I do believe you're blushing," said Margaret. *"Pourquoi?"*

"Ferme-la, Marguerite." I slide back into the booth and glare at Raf. "So, were *you* dancing like that?"

He laughs. "I only danced a couple of times. The music mostly blew, so me and my friends just hung out. Some of *your* friends, though, whoa! They were going wild in there."

"Like whom?" Margaret asks. "No, wait. Don't tell me. I don't want to know. Okay, tell me. Was it

Leigh Ann?" I knew Margaret would figure out a way to bring her up.

"No, she was pretty cool. This other girl, though— long blond hair, kinda tall—*she* was totally out of control."

"Oh my God. Bridget. It has to be," I say.

"It was like she'd just been let out of an all-female prison after a looonnnnng stretch."

I hold up my hand. "Oy. Stop. Let's change the subject while I still have a tiny morsel of respect for my lesser friend."

Margaret sets the copy of the letter on the table. "Number three. Ms. Sophie, this one's all yours."

"Me? Why me?"

"Because you, my dear, are our resident math whiz. We got the religion clue and the classical language clue."

"Okay. Let me see. 612 divided by D, which is the distance between the centers of the south and west rose windows. What am I missing?"

"What's a rose window?" Raf asks.

"Oh, come on," says Margaret. "The big round windows on the ends of the church? They look like flowers, hence the name *rose* window. There are three in St. Veronica's." She opens her notebook up to a blank page and (using a ruler, naturally) draws the church in outline form:

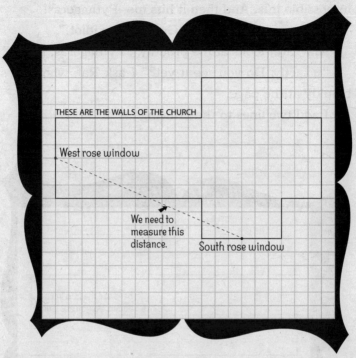

THESE ARE THE WALLS OF THE CHURCH

West rose window

We need to
measure this
distance.

South rose window

"Okay, the church looks like a big cross, right? The two rose windows we're concerned with are here and here." She marks Xs on the south and west walls. "Are you with me so far, Raf?"

"Um, yeah."

"Well, to find this distance he calls D, all we have to do is measure from here to here."

"But those windows are like a hundred feet off the ground, and there are two walls in the way." I take the pen and draw a (more or less) straight line from the center of the south façade to the center of the west façade, thinking I am about to prove to Margaret how utterly impossible it is. And then it hits me. Pythagoras!

"This is easy!" I rave. "God, I'm an idiot."

Margaret looks at me proudly. "Pythagoras, right?"

"Exactly. Do you see it yet?" I ask Raf, who stares blankly at the page.

I add two lines to the drawing:

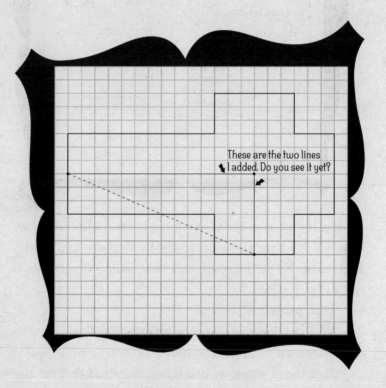

These are the two lines I added. Do you see it yet?

"It's a triangle. A *right* triangle."

Raf can only shake his head. "No idea what you're talking about."

"Sophie, kindly explain the Pythagorean theorem to our dimmish friend here."

Boy, am I smart.

"Pythagoras was a Greek mathematician, and here's what he figured out. See, here's a right triangle. We'll call the sides A, B, and C.

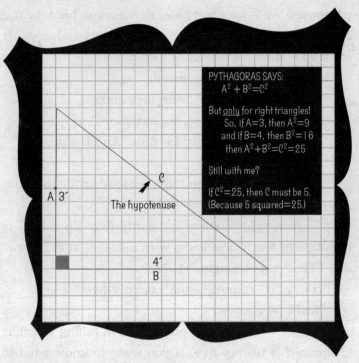

PYTHAGORAS SAYS:
$$A^2 + B^2 = C^2$$

But <u>only</u> for right triangles!
So, if A=3, then A^2=9
and if B=4, then B^2=16
then $A^2+B^2=C^2$=25

Still with me?

If C^2=25, then C must be 5.
(Because 5 squared=25.)

A 3´

C

The hypotenuse

4´
B

"This corner down here between the A and B is our right angle, okay? The long side, side C, is called the hypotenuse. It's always opposite, or across from, the right angle. In other words, the side that is the hypotenuse is never a part of the right angle. With me? Good. Our friend Pythagoras figured out this rule that's always true about right triangles. Any right triangle. Doesn't matter how big or what the other two angles are, as long as one angle in the triangle is ninety degrees. Let's say that side A is three feet long, and side B is four feet, okay, and what we want to know is, how long is side C, our hypotenuse? Well, we don't have to measure, because the Pythagorean theorem says that A squared plus B squared equals C squared. It's easy."

Raf does *not* look convinced.

"What's A squared?" Margaret quizzes.

"A squared? A is three, so, um, nine."

"That's right. A squared is nine. And B squared?"

"Sixteen."

"Right." I urge him on. "So, remember the formula. A squared plus B squared—"

"So, nine plus sixteen is twenty-five. So side C is twenty-five feet?" Raf looks with disbelief at the drawing. "That can't be right."

"It's not. C *squared* equals twenty-five," I say.

"Yes?" he guesses.

I giggle. "That's not a question. I'm telling you that C *squared* is twenty-five. If you want to know what C is, you need the square root of twenty-five. Which is . . ." I wait. And wait.

"Five?"

"Yes!"

"You can measure it if you want to," Margaret adds,

"but trust me, it works. It's been around for *thousands* of years. The three-four-five right triangle is the easiest, but you can use the same principle for *any* right triangle. If one of the angles is ninety degrees, and you know the lengths of the two short sides, you can always figure out the length of the third—the hypotenuse."

"Yeah, so look at the drawing of the church again." I push it under his nose.

Raf examines the drawing carefully. "So what you're saying is, if we measure from here to here, and here to here, we can figure out, using this Pyth—this formula of yours, how far it is from here to here, even though there are walls in the way."

"That's *exactly* what we're saying. Pretty cool, huh?" Margaret gives him a little shove.

"What about the fact that the windows are forty feet up?" He looks smug, certain that he has discovered the flaw in our reasoning.

"It doesn't matter, O simple one," I say. "The distance is the same, whether we're measuring at the bottom of the wall or the top. I think it's safe to assume that the walls are vertical and that the windows are the same height. So, do you believe me now?"

"Do I *believe* you?" Raf asks. "About what?"

"About whether we can solve this clue using Pythagoras."

"Um. Sure. Why not?"

"Good, because it's all up to you now. While you two

were getting pizza, I did a little measuring in the church." Margaret flips to a new page in her notebook and starts writing. She sets up the whole problem for Raf and spins the notebook for him to see. "Here are the dimensions for your side A and your side B. It's all yours, sport."

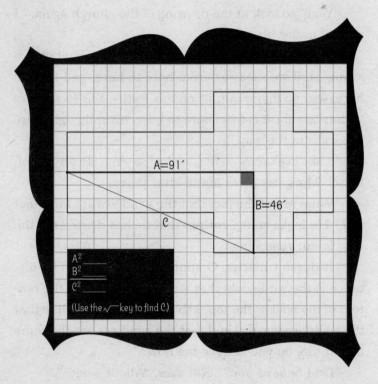

A=91′

B=46′

C

A^2 _____
B^2 _____
C^2 _____

(Use the $\sqrt{}$ key to find C.)

Chapter 19

Don't read this chapter until you have
solved the problem in the previous chapter
yourself. Seriously. Just think how shiny-
clever you'll feel when you've aced it

The floor of the church, it turns out, is covered with
stone tiles that are *exactly* twelve inches by twelve
inches, with virtually no space between them. Who
knew? Besides Margaret, that is. She told me later that
she noticed the floor tiles on our way out of the church,
so, while she sent Raf and me off to Ray's, she made certain they really were twelve-inch tiles and then counted
them. From the back wall of the church, directly under
the rose window, to the center line of the transept is exactly ninety-one feet, and from the center point of the
transept to the south wall is exactly forty-six feet.

Margaret and I watch and say nothing as Raf does
the calculations.

"Okay, we have one side of the triangle that is 91

feet. 91 times 91 equals 8,281. The other side is 46 feet. 46 squared is 2,116," he says, punching it all in on Margaret's cell phone.

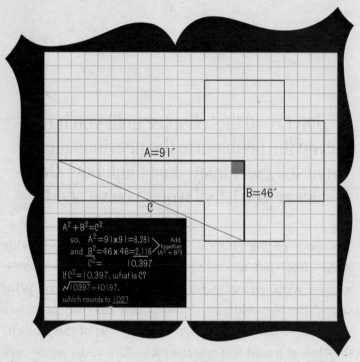

A=91´

B=46´

C

$A^2 + B^2 = C^2$

so. $A^2 = 91 \times 91 = 8,281$

and $B^2 = 46 \times 46 = 2,116$

Add together ($A^2 + B^2$)

$C^2 = 10,397$

If $C^2 = 10,397$. what is C?

$\sqrt{10397} = 101.97$.

which rounds to 102´

"That's A squared and B squared, right?" says Raf, mastering his Pythagoras after all. "So now what? Wait, don't tell me! I remember this part. Add them together, right? A squared plus B squared."

"So far, so good," says Margaret. "You're on a roll, pretty boy."

Raf grins and plunges right in. "8,281 plus 2,116, that's 10,397." He looks up triumphantly. "AHA!"

"You're not done yet," I say.

He frowns. "Square root of that?"

"Yep."

He punches it in. "The square root of 10,397 is 101.96568."

Margaret takes a look at the screen. "Which, rounded to the nearest foot, is 102."

"So that's it? It's 102 feet from this window to that one." Raf points at the diagram. "Are you sure? It seems almost *too* easy."

"It *is* easy if you know the secret formula," Margaret teases. "But you're *still* not quite done."

"That's right," I say. "You've got the answer for D, which is the *distance* between the windows, but there's still one more step to find the clue."

As Raf examines the paper, a cloud of confusion comes over his face. "What are you talking about? You said—oh, wait. I get it. To get the final answer, it's 612 *divided by* 102. Give me the phone." He punches in the numbers and holds up the answer for us to see.

"Six. That's kind of amazing that it came out to be a whole number like that, don't you think?"

"Well, it definitely makes me think we got it right," Margaret says. "Obviously, he set the problem up that way on purpose—making it easy with the floor tiles and working it out ahead of time so it comes out with a nice round number like six. This also means that we have the first half of the problem done already. See how easy that was, once we set our minds to it? The first equation is $X + 3Y = 6$. Right?"

And then I see the look—and this time it is *way* beyond that hundred-watt-bulb-over-the-head look. She is onto something *huge,* and frankly, she is scaring the kajeepers out of me. See, Mr. Eliot told me about this Mr. Krook character in Charles Dickens's novel *Bleak House,* who spontaneously combusts, leaving behind nothing but a smelly, greasy spot on the floor. I swear that's going to happen to Margaret Wrobel one day. She's going to be thinking really hard, with her hands over her ears, and then—poof!—she'll just burst into flames right before my eyes.

I'm also starting to believe Mr. E's theory that *whatever* the life question, Dickens has an answer.

Chapter 20

In which I play with feeling and actually enjoy a crosstown bus ride

Yikes! I almost forgot about my guitar lesson, which I have every Saturday at five o'clock. It is almost four when we leave the church for the last time, and I still have to go home, grab my guitar, and catch a crosstown bus to the West Side. I haven't practiced much during the week and I have to get my butt in gear.

Margaret is serious about her music and totally understands my commitment to the guitar and my dream of superstardom, and Raf looks like he's had about enough intrigue for one day, so we jump on the subway at Sixty-eighth and head for Ninety-sixth Street. Raf agrees to wait and take the bus across town with me—is that weird? When we get to my apartment, he throws himself onto the sofa while I run into my bedroom and zip my guitar into its carrying case.

"Where is everybody? I haven't seen your parents in a long time. How's your dad doin' anyway? He's kinda cool."

My dad? Cool? On what planet? "Um, I don't know. I guess Dad's at work, and Mom's probably teaching a lesson. They're fine; I'm sure they're just like they were the last time you saw them. They're parents—they don't change."

"And they trust you here alone?" he says as I saunter into the living room, guitar strapped to my back.

"Uh, yeah, I guess. It's not like they're never here. One of them is practically *always* here. Are you ready? What's the time?"

"Four-thirty-five. Plenty of time."

"C'mon. Let's go, let's go. I don't wanna be late."

Raf slowly pulls himself off the sofa and we are on our way. I have the weirdest feeling that he doesn't want to leave—that he wants to stay and hang out with . . . me? When I mention it to Margaret later, she doesn't try to discourage me or anything, but she says that it could just be because he's a lazy, lazy boy.

We get seats together on the bus and because of the way that guys sprawl across seats on the bus or subway, my leg is against his for the entire trip. I've never been so eager *and* reluctant to get off a bus in my life.

Somehow, my lesson *rocks*. Even Gerry (I can teach you guitar in 12 EZ lessons!) notices the difference. "You're playing with a lot of *feeling* today, Sophie. What's going on? Are you in love or something?"

I blush for the second time that day. God! "N-no. I'm not in *love*."

"Hey, it's okay if you are. Love is a good thing for musicians. Next to practice, it's probably the most important thing."

When I get home after my lesson, Mom doesn't feel like cooking, so she takes me out for Chinese—General Tso's Chicken. My fortune cookie promises "romance from an unexpected source." Yay!

As long as I don't get into too much trouble and keep my grades up, *and* practice my guitar, my mom is pretty easygoing. When she asks what I have been doing all day, I can't tell her *everything*, but I try not to out-and-out lie. Is leaving out some of the truth the same as lying? I suppose that if I had told her we'd been to a nightclub, a tattoo parlor, and a Wicca convention, she would have asked more questions. But a museum, a coffee shop, and a church? C'mon, how wholesome can you get?

We stop at Blockbuster on the way home and pick up a light and fizzy romantic comedy. I am *so* looking forward to a lazy, mellow evening at home, curled up on the couch with Mom, eating popcorn and watching the movie. And then the phone rings.

Chapter 21

Oh my God. We're learning new math concepts on a Saturday night

"Where have you been!" Margaret scolds. "We've been trying to call you for hours."

"You have?" I check my cell phone, and sure enough, it's dead. "Oops."

"Well, you have to get over here."

"Now?" The opening credits are still rolling on the movie. That couch looks mighty inviting.

"Yeah, now. My parents took my grandmother out to dinner and then to a concert, so I actually have my room all to myself. Becca and Leigh Ann are already here."

"They are? Jeez."

"So, you coming?"

"Umm . . ." The movie is starting, and Mom looks over at me.

"Go," she says. "You're not going to hurt my feelings."

"Are you sure?" The slightest hesitation on her part, and I have a perfectly valid reason to quietly vegetate for a few hours.

"I'm sure."

Heavy sigh.

"I'll be there in ten."

Margaret actually has an enormous message board—the kind you can write on with different-colored markers—in her bedroom. She keeps track of her assignments and her responsibilities at home, and her parents leave her messages on it. She has cleared all that stuff away and in its place has drawn the following diagram:

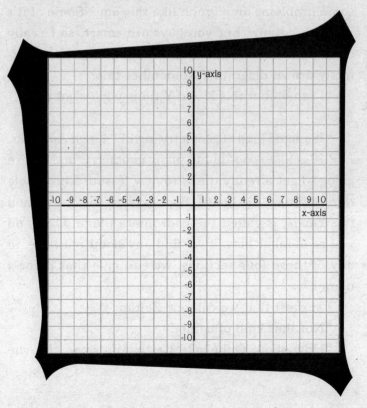

"Now before anybody freaks out on me, this isn't homework. I figured something out really important about the puzzle. It took me a while to put it all together, but I've got it."

She sits Rebecca, Leigh Ann, and me down on the edge of her bed while she starts right in on her lesson. (Wasting time is frowned upon in Sister Margaret's classroom.)

"You should remember at least part of this from last year. Remember, at the end of the year we did some problems on a graph like this one? Some of it's going to be new, but you guys are smart, so I really don't think it will be that hard." She points at her perfectly drawn diagram. "Remember this?"

"I remember this X and Y thing you've got there," I say.

"It's some kind of geometry, right?" Leigh Ann asks.

"It's called coordinate plane geometry, and you're going to get a really quick review lesson. This whole *thing* here on the board, Sophie, with the X-axis and the Y-axis, is called the coordinate plane. Okay, do you remember how, if we find any point out here, in any of these four sections, we can give that point a name?"

I suggest that we call one Zoltan.

"Not that kind of name."

"How about Ophelia?" Leigh Ann says. "Maybe they're girls."

"I think I'll name mine . . . Frodo," says Rebecca, a huge *Lord of the Rings* freak. With the red marker, she makes a dime-size dot on the board, taps it with her outstretched finger. "I dub thee . . . Sir Frodo the point."

Margaret draws an empty set of parentheses next to Frodo. "Actually, children, we use two *numbers* to name every point. The first number is the distance you travel on the X-axis away from the 'zero point' in the sideways direction, either to the right or to the left. The second is the distance you travel on the Y-axis away from zero. So, using Frodo here as an example, you start at the zero point—and you count. One, two, three, four along the X-axis. So the first part of the 'name' of this point is four." She writes the number four inside the parentheses.

"That one is called the X-coordinate. Then you have to go up—and see, now we're moving in the Y-axis direction, up and down—one, two, three, and you're there. So, the second number in the name is called the Y-coordinate." She writes a 3 in the parentheses next to the 4, so she has (4,3) next to the Point Formerly Known as Frodo.

It is all starting to come back to me. "And you can do negative numbers, too, right?"

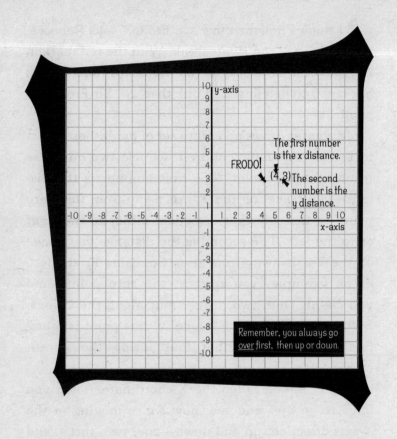

Margaret nods enthusiastically. "Absolutely." She writes (-4,2) at the top of the board. "Where is this point? And remember, you *always* go in the X direction first. You go left if it's negative and right if it's positive."

I stand and count out four spaces to the left, and then move up two and make another red dot. "Right here."

"Perfect! You even went the right direction on the

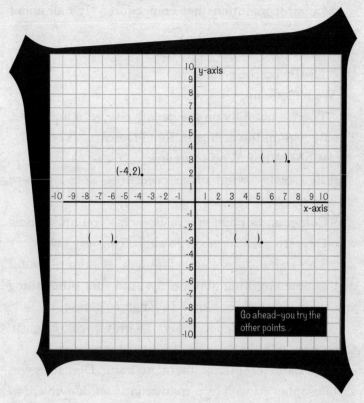

Y-axis. On the Y-axis, positive numbers are up, and negative numbers are down. All right, so far, so good. Any questions?"

I raise my hand. "Um, Miss Wrobel, don't get me wrong, I'm having fun in your class, and you're learnin' me *reeeal* good—but what does all this have to do with the puzzle?"

"A *just* question," says Rebecca, nodding solemnly at me.

Margaret maintains her composure. "It's all about the fly."

"What fly?" Leigh Ann asks.

"The fly on the *ceiling*."

We all look up.

"There's not a fly on the ceiling *now,* you imbeciles. The fly was on the ceiling in René Descartes's room."

"Who? Who? Who?" we ask.

Flies, owls—what other creatures were in there with us?

"Come on. Sophie, you're French—you must know who Descartes is. *Cogito ergo sum.* Ring any bells?"

"The name does sound familiar," I admit, "but I don't know anything about a fly. And that other thing you said—just tell us, okay? In English, please."

"Yes, please," Rebecca says. "I only speak English, Cantonese, a little Spanish, and text-messaging."

"It's Latin for 'I think, therefore I am.' Descartes was a philosopher as well as a mathematician. He *invented* the coordinate plane. The story goes that one day he was lying in bed staring at a fly on the ceiling and became obsessed with being able to describe the motion of the fly as it walked around."

Jeez, when I'm staring at the ceiling, I'm usually trying to figure out the lyrics to a song, or whether I should start plucking my eyebrows and how much it's going to hurt—it never involves higher mathematics or philosophy.

Rebecca raises her hand. "Um, Margaret? Can we get back to Zoltan's question? What the *hell* does this have to do with this ring of power we're trying to find?"

Margaret laughs. "The letter. Caroline's grandfather was telling her, in his way, that to solve the puzzle she needed to use the coordinate plane. Listen to what he says at the end of the letter: *'sometimes in life the most difficult problems are solved by lying in bed and staring at that seemingly insignificant fly on the ceiling.'* "

My eyes dart back and forth from Margaret to the whiteboard. "It's like a treasure map!"

"Basically. The clues are leading us to points on the floor of the church. The lines between the floor tiles make up a *perfect* coordinate plane. I'll show you."

She turns back to the whiteboard and takes marker in hand. "This part is a little harder to explain, but trust me, it's not that hard, and once you see what I'm doing, well, you'll see—this whole puzzle is not nearly as difficult as we thought. Once I realized that the puzzle had something to do with the coordinate plane, I knew I was going to need Mr. Kessel's help. I remembered from math camp last summer that there was something about equations and graphing, but I couldn't remember how to do it. So, while you were off at your guitar lesson, I sent

Mr. Kessel an e-mail. I figured, what's he going to be doing on a Saturday afternoon? He doesn't strike me as the college football type. Probably online, right?"

"What *does* Mr. Kessel do on the weekends?" Rebecca asks. "Hang out with other math geeks, solving equations or something?"

I nudge her. "Hey, Rebecca—shhhhhhhh. Look around you. What are *you* doing?"

"Well, I must have been right about him being online because he wrote back to me in under ten minutes, and he sent me a link to a site that explained it all. I suppose I could just show you guys the site, but this is more fun, and I think I can explain it better."

"Did Kessel ask why you wanted to know?" Rebecca seems skeptical that a teacher might be willing to help us out without some shady ulterior motive.

"Yeah, he was super-nice. I told him I was working on a math puzzle. He said to e-mail him if I got stuck and he'd help me out. He's not as bad as you guys think. He's funny!"

Leigh Ann agrees with Margaret. "I heard that he used to do stand-up comedy."

"Mr. Kessel?" Rebecca asks. "He always looks at me like he's disappointed or something. Just because I'm Asian, everybody thinks I should be good at math."

"Everyone does *not* think that, Becca," I say.

"Asians are good at math?" Leigh Ann asks.

Point made.

Margaret continues with her lesson. "It's not just individual points like these that you can graph out on the coordinate plane, you can also graph *lines* and *equations*. For example, let's take a very simple equation." She writes $X + Y = 4$ on the board and then draws two columns, one labeled X and the other Y. "Sophie, pick a number for X. Any number."

"Two."

"Okay, Rebecca, if X is two, what does Y *have* to be in order to make this equation true? In other words, two plus *what* equals four?"

"Two?"

"Right! So there's one point. If X is two and Y is two, our pair is . . ." She wrote a two in the X column and a 2 in the Y column. "Now, give me a couple more numbers for X."

"Three and six," I volunteer.

"Good. If X is three, Y must be one, right?" She adds those numbers to the columns. "You *have* to make the equation true, so X plus Y *always* has to equal four. How about for six? What do you add to six to get four?"

"You can't," says Rebecca. "You have to subtract. No, wait, that's wrong. You can add a *negative* number. Same thing. Six plus negative two equals four."

"Exactly! So, now we have three pairs of numbers."
The whiteboard looks like this:

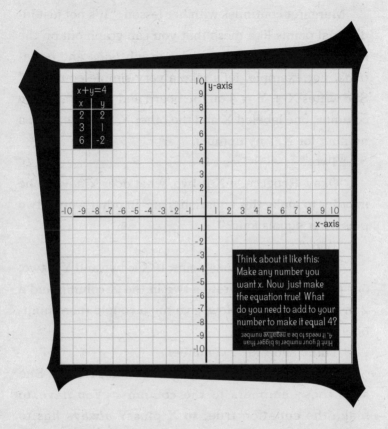

"Now watch what happens when we plot those points on our coordinate plane." She quickly marks our three points in red. Then she places a yardstick against the whiteboard so that it hits all three dots and draws a line.

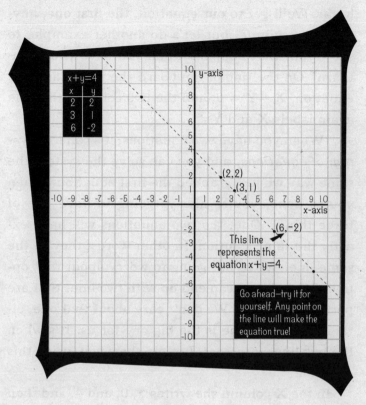

"This *line* now represents the equation X plus Y equals four. Pretty cool, huh? And you see, no matter what numbers you use for X and Y, as long as they make the equation true, those *points* will always fall right on this line."

"I see that," Rebecca says. "This *is* cool."

"I know," Margaret agrees. "But wait, it gets better. The next step is when you have *two* equations, which is what we just *happen* to have in this letter. We'll get to our equation, the first one, any-way, in a minute, but let's do another example, to show you what happens when you have two equa-tions." On the side of the board she writes another equation, $X - Y = 0$, and the two columns that she again labels X and Y.

"When you have two equations, it's called a *system of equations,* and you can solve the system the same way we just graphed the first equation. When you're done, you're always going to have one of three things. One, the two equations will have ex-actly the same solution. In other words, they're the same line. We're not going to worry about that op-tion. Second, you can end up with two lines that are perfectly parallel. We don't care about that one, ei-ther. The third one is the big one for us. It's when the two lines *intersect.* Let me show you, using this equation."

In the X column she writes 2, 0, and 4, and then writes the same numbers in the Y column. "Are you with me? If X minus Y equals 0, then X and Y are always going to be the same, right? Now we graph these points and draw the line for that equa-tion."

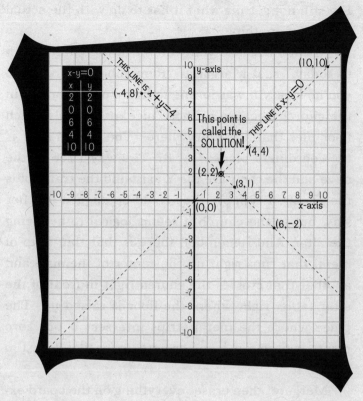

"See, the line for this equation intersects the line for our first equation at this *one* point. This point, (2,2), is the *solution* to this system of equations. It is the *only* point that occurs on both lines." For emphasis, she draws over the two lines several times, making a distinct X. "Now, do you remember what Raf said?"

"X marks the spot," I say. "I think I've seen this in a movie."

"I understand all this stuff," says Leigh Ann, "but

I'm still not getting what it has to do with the actual *finding* of anything."

"That's because you weren't in the church with us today," said Margaret. "Remember, Soph, I told you how easy it was for me to figure out distances in the church because of those nice, neat twelve-inch floor tiles that are everywhere? The church *floor* is the coordinate plane. Get it? The way I see it, the nave and the choir are the Y-axis, and the transept is the X-axis. I suppose they could be aligned another way, but in the church it seems logical to be facing the altar. And remember, there is that thin strip of metal that runs right up the center of the aisle and another that crosses the church right in front of the altar table, right where the floor is raised up. The place where the metal strips intersect is our zero point, and the ring is somewhere *under* that floor. I'm sure of it."

Margaret then erases everything on the board except the X-axis and the Y-axis. To one side, she writes the equation $X + 3Y = 6$ and then steps back. "Okay, Sophie, this one's all yours. This is what we have so far—the answers from the first three clues. Plot the line for that equation."

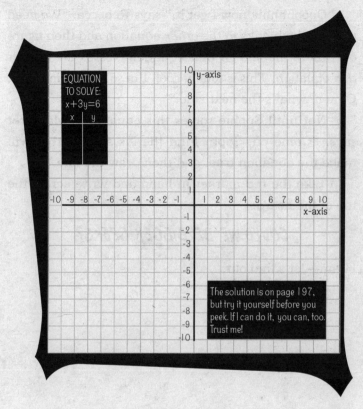

EQUATION
TO SOLVE:
x+3y=6

x	y

y-axis

x-axis

The solution is on page 197,
but try it yourself before you
peek. If I can do it, you can, too.
Trust me!

I am suddenly very tingly. "You mean that's it? All I have to do is draw the line that fits this equation, and we'll know where the ring is?"

"It's not quite *that* easy, Soph. Yes, we will know that the hiding place is somewhere on the line, but we won't know *where* on the line, which could be ninety feet long. And even if some of the tiles are loose, most of them probably aren't, and I doubt that Father Danahey would appreciate us digging up the entire church floor."

"Oooohhhhh, now I get it," says Rebecca. "We need to fill in the blanks in the *other* equation and then figure out where the line for *that* equation crosses the line for *this* equation. This is totally cool. I'm so getting into this. C'mon, what's the next clue?"

"Not until Sophie solves this equation," Margaret says. "Come on, Soph. Find the Xs and Ys that will make the equation true, and then draw the line."

I take the red marker in hand and write across the top of the board:

COULD WE BE BIGGER GEEKS?

Hmm—let's find out.

Chapter 22

In which, as hard as this may be to believe, new heights (depths?) of geekdom are reached

Sadly, the answer to my question is a resounding yes. It's not like junior high kids in New York have these amazing social lives (at least, not the people I know), but come on, we are sitting in front of a whiteboard in Margaret's apartment learning new math concepts. On a *Saturday* night.

I call an official time-out from the Xs and Ys because I need to hear about Rebecca's afternoon in Chelsea with Ms. Harriman. (I am also dying to hear Leigh Ann's version of events from the dance, but I don't want to be the one to ask.)

"What was she wearing? Another cowgirl wedding dress?" Leigh Ann asks.

"She went with more of a Goth look this time. It was a long, lacy black dress with a spider web in the back. I almost didn't recognize her because she had her hair all pulled up under a hat. And she had black gloves on—up to her elbows!"

"How about the shoes?"

"Black Chuck Taylors. I kid you not."

"All right! Chucks *rule.*" I just happen to be wearing a red pair.

"So I show up at this gallery, and there's like a million people because it's the opening of a show for some artist whose paintings I don't get at all, and I swear Elizabeth knows everybody. The mayor's there, and some rapper I've never heard of, and a couple of the Yankees. And she's introducing me to everybody like *I'm* her long-lost daughter, and I feel like a total schlub with my stupid sketchbook that I am just *praying* she doesn't ask me to show to these people."

"Did she?" I ask, cringing.

"No, thank God. After about an hour, the place empties out—like *that*—and we go into her friend Alessandra's office. She owns the gallery and is like the total opposite of Ms. Harriman. She's wearing this chic little black dress, perfectly normal. So, Ms. Harriman tells her about meeting all of us, and how impressed she is with my drawings, blah, blah, blah, and this lady— Alessandra—takes a look at them, and, and . . . she likes them, too! She wants me to come there for this special program for supposedly gifted young artists—for free!"

"Oh my gosh. That is great, Becca," says Margaret. "When do you start?"

"In a couple of weeks. She showed me the studio upstairs. It's amazing. Every year, she finds about ten kids and brings in friends of hers who are artists to do the teaching. I saw some of the things they're working on, and wow! I can't wait."

"What did your mom say?" I ask.

"I haven't told her yet." Suddenly the excitement drains out of her face and she falls backward onto the bed. "Oh, man. My mom's job. I'm not gonna be able to do it."

"What!" cries Leigh Ann.

"What *about* your mom's job? Did she change shifts?" Margaret asks, very concerned.

"It's not just that, she's—" I blurt out before remembering my promise not to tell.

"She's *what*?" Margaret has me by the arm.

"Sorry, but I'm telling them, Becca."

So I spill. Even the part about her possibly leaving St. Veronica's.

"That's completely unacceptable," Margaret declares. "Did you tell Elizabeth about all this?"

"No way," says Rebecca. "Why?"

"Because, people like Elizabeth Harriman can make things happen," Margaret declares. "Look at you— you're twelve years old and on your way in the New York art scene."

"My mom would *kill* me if I told a complete stranger about family stuff."

"She's not a *complete* stranger," I say.

"She is a little *strange,* though," says Leigh Ann.

Rebecca waves both arms at us. "Everybody stop! I don't want to think about it anymore. Let's talk about somebody else's problems. C'mon, Sophie, *you* must have a problem."

"Nope. Not a one. Everything's perfect." *Did Margaret tell her my secret about you-know-who?*

Before anyone has the chance to go nosing around in my life, Leigh Ann stands and takes charge. "I have a better idea. Why don't we work on our skit for the Dickens banquet? We're all here; if we put our heads together, we can write our script tonight, and we'll have a week to practice. I want to *win* this thing."

"Win?" I ask. "It's a contest?"

"Of course. The best solo act and the best skit win prizes."

"Books, Sophie," says Margaret. "For your collection. Dickens. Hardcovers."

Ooooohhhh. I rub my hands together.

"I already have a good scene in mind," says Leigh Ann. "It's from chapter twenty-seven, where Joe comes to visit Pip in London."

"I'm only up to chapter twenty," I say.

"I've read about twenty *pages,*" said Rebecca. "And don't include me in this, anyway. My mom wants me home right after school every day to babysit, so she doesn't have to pay for day care, and besides, I doubt I can go to the banquet this Friday."

Leigh Ann isn't giving in that easily. "You can be Biddy. It's a small part. And you don't have to memorize it. You can read your lines, because it's supposed to be a letter that she writes to Pip. It's perfect. Come on!"

Rebecca slaps her palm to her forehead. "Aaaiiiiyyyyy."

Margaret shakes her head at her. "When are you going to learn, Rebecca? We *never* give up. We're permanent. Like a tattoo. Attached, like leeches."

"So, what's the scene about?" I ask. "Give me the SparkNotes version."

Leigh Ann explains. "Pip gets a letter from Biddy telling him that Joe is coming to visit, and Pip is kind of bummed, because he's afraid Joe will embarrass him. Joe shows up and has dinner with Pip and Herbert, and . . . oh, you'll see. It's really funny, but it's also kind of sad."

"You know, classic Dickens," Margaret adds.

Now to the nitty-gritty. "And who am I?"

"I was thinking you could be Pip's roommate, Herbert," says Leigh Ann. "Margaret can be Pip, and I'll be Joe. I mean, if that's all right with you guys. I don't want you to think I'm taking things over. I know I'm still the new girl."

Margaret pats her on the back. "It's *good* that you're taking charge. I've been kind of preoccupied with this puzzle, and, um, other stuff that's going on here. We haven't even thought about the skit."

"How are things going with your grandmother, anyway? Any better?" I ask.

Margaret sighs. " 'Bout the same. It's just—well, let me give an example from this morning. Mom asked me to go out to Gristedes for some milk, so I asked Babcia—that's my grandmother—if she wanted to go with me. We hardly get out the door, and she's stopping at every garbage can on the block, looking for empty cans and bottles. Somehow she found out that they're worth a nickel apiece, and she's telling me how in Poland, she could live on what the people in my building throw away."

"She's probably right," Rebecca says.

"Yeah, but some of our neighbors saw us, and I wanted to crawl under a parked car."

"Aww, she's just from a different world, Margaret," says Leigh Ann.

"I know, I know. I mean, when I think of what she's been through—the Depression, the war, the Holocaust, communism—I'd probably be the same way. But she's still embarrassing."

"Well, are you sure you're okay playing Pip in this skit?" Leigh Ann asks. "Because, you know, he's—" She stops herself, smiling ever so slightly.

Margaret moves to her computer. "Absolutely. You talk, I'll type. And while I get set up, tell us all about the dance."

My ears and everything else perk up.

"Oh, I didn't stay that long," Leigh Ann starts. "Not that many kids from St. V's were there—but that girl

Bridget . . ." Her big, beautiful, dramatic eyes widen. "She is *wild.*"

Without looking up from the keyboard, Margaret says, "Raf told us that part."

Leigh Ann instantly smiles at the mention of Raf's name. "Oh, yeah, I ended up hanging with him and his friends for a while—he's funny—"

Grrrrrr. He's *funny?*

"—and so nice. And he's *really* cute."

Just kill me now. Please. Get it all over with.

"So, what's his deal, anyway? Is he, you know—"

"Available?" Margaret asks without looking up from the computer.

Leigh Ann gives us kind of a shy shrug. "Um, yeah, I guess."

Margaret turns to face me. "I don't know. What do *you* think, Soph? *Is* Raf available?"

I stammer for a second, and then a voice that comes from somewhere inside my amoeba-size brain says, "As far as I know."

Leigh Ann's dimples deepen. "Good to know."

I am stupid, stupid, stupid.

Chapter 23

In which we learn that teachers are actually human beings. Who knew?

On Sunday mornings, Dad makes me my favorite breakfast of crepes with Nutella and bananas, along with this totally decadent coffee, chocolate, and whipped cream concoction that he *claims* he invented. After a night of tossing and turning imagining Leigh Ann and Raf having a fabulous time at the dance, it is just what I need. She thinks he's *funny. Grrrr,* again.

Dad sets a perfectly folded crepe on my plate and my mind drifts back to the museum and the legend of the ring.

"Dad, what's the name of the town where you grew up?"

"Ste. Croix du Mont. *Pourquoi, mon petit chou-chou?*"

I giggle. I love it when he calls me his "little cabbage."

"Oh, I'm just wondering. Me and Margaret are

doing this project. Have you ever heard of a place called Rocamadour?"

"Ah, *oui*. It is maybe one hundred kilometers east of Ste. Croix du Mont. A very famous place."

"Do you know anything about some rings from there? With special powers, supposedly."

"Of course. *Les bagues de Rocamadour?* St. Veronica, like your school, *n'est-ce pas?*"

"That's right! So, it's true? The legend, I mean?"

Mom lowers the Arts section of the Sunday *New York Times*. She looks quizzical. "What legend?"

"The rings were a gift from Veronica," I begin. "You know, from the Bible. They're wedding rings, and—"

"Legend says that if a person wears the ring and prays to St. Veronica, she will appear in a dream and will answer their prayers," Dad finishes.

"Nice. And *where* is this ring?"

"One of them is in the Met," I say. "But that's the man's ring. The other one is, well, that's what we're kind of trying to find out."

"It disappeared a long time ago," Dad says. "There are many theories, but no one knows for sure where it is. Probably still on someone's finger, dead and buried."

Or in a church on the Upper East Side.

"Mom, if the ring was for real, and you had it, what would you wish for?"

"Sophie, it is not a wishing well." Dad takes his legends seriously.

"All right, what would you *pray* for?" I stick out my tongue at Dad.

"Nothing. I have everything I need right here at this table."

Geez—that is *such* a Mom answer.

It is a perfect New York City September afternoon. After I finish breakfast, I go to meet Margaret's babcia. The doorman lets me go up without buzzing the Wrobels. Outside their apartment door, I hear Margaret playing the violin, so I wait until she gets to the end of the piece. After the clapping and the shouts of "Encore!" I knock quickly.

Mr. Wrobel answers the door. "Sophie! So good to see you! Come in, come in. Margaret is entertaining us with a little Chopin. He was Polish, you know."

"Um, yeah, I think I heard that. It sounded *great,* Margaret."

"One day soon—Carnegie Hall!" Mr. Wrobel practically shouts.

"Papa! That's a long way off. Besides, Sophie doesn't want to hear you bragging about me, do you, Soph?"

"Ummm, no, it's okay. He's right, you'll be playing in Carnegie Hall, and I'll be in some smoky dive in the East Village."

Mr. Wrobel pulls me into the living room, where Margaret's mom and grandmother sit in matching wing chairs. "This is my mother." He says something to her in Polish; I catch my name and Margaret's.

She smiles politely at me. "Sophie," she says softly.

I smile back. "Hi."

Awkward silence.

Somebody else, *please* say something. English, Polish, Swahili, Klingon, anything.

Margaret's mom finally asks me how I like the upper school and how my parents are—typical parent questions, to which I give her the typical kid responses: "It's okay" and "Oh, they're fine."

Margaret rescues me by dragging me back to her room.

"Let's go out," I suggest. "It's beautiful."

"Yeah, I know. We went to the early Mass," she says. "So, what do you want to do?"

"I dunno. I was thinking about a movie, but it's *way* too nice. Maybe we should go hang in the park. You can bring a book if you want. I just didn't want to stick around the house. My mom woulda had me cleaning my room or something."

"Hmmm. That might be a good thing."

"*That's* beside the point. So that's your grandmother, huh? She doesn't seem that bad to me."

"I never said she was *bad*. I said she was driving me bananas."

"Well, she seems nice to me."

"Sophie, you've known her for two seconds. Go for a

walk around the block with her, then tell me what you think. Or take the subway. Yesterday she started *singing*—in Polish—on the train."

"I seem to remember that you *liked* singing with her."

"Past tense. I was six."

"C'mon, let's go. We can call Rebecca later. Maybe she can sneak out for a while."

Margaret digs into her book bag, excavating her copy of *Great Expectations*. "What about Leigh Ann? Should we call her?"

I respond with a typical parent answer. "Maybe later."

We enter Central Park at Ninety-seventh Street and find a nice spot to read and soak up the sun on the rocks near the ball fields in the North Meadow. Rebecca shows up about forty-five minutes later, sketchbook in hand and dressed in all black. We tease her about taking the whole artiste thing a little too seriously, which leads us to Ms. Harriman, which leads to the fourth clue. And guess what? Margaret *just happens* to have a sheet of paper on which she has printed the clue in great big letters.

It says:

ONE OF THE FOLLOWING CHARACTERS DOESN'T BELONG IN THIS LIST:

DRUMMLE, GUPPY, HEEP, STEERFORTH,
TRADDLES, PIRRIP, SUMMERSON, SQUEERS,
COPPERFIELD, SCROOGE

THAT CHARACTER'S FIRST NAME IS THE
SAME AS THE LAST NAME OF SOMEONE
WHO DONATED A SINGLE CHURCH PEW.
LOOK BEHIND THE BRASS PLAQUE THAT
BEARS THAT NAME.

"I've heard of David Copperfield, and I know
Scrooge," Rebecca says, "but who the hell are all these
other people?"

"I *think* they're all from Charles Dickens's books, but
I'm not a hundred percent sure," says Margaret. "I've only
read *David Copperfield* (Harvard Classics, fiction, volumes
seven and eight) and now, part of *Great Expectations*
(which, much to Mr. Eliot's dismay, is *not* included in the
Harvard Classics). And by the way, you know Pirrip, too."

"I do?"

"That's Pip. His real name is Philip Pirrip, remember?"

"And I know Drummle, too," I say. "He's the guy
Pip hates. Jaggers calls him the spider. Bentley is his
first name."

"And *Uriah* Heep, *Thomas* Traddles, *James* Steerforth, and *David* Copperfield, obviously, are all from

David Copperfield," Margaret adds. "Which leaves us with . . . Guppy, Summerson, and Squeers that we don't know anything about."

"We can fix that in like five minutes if we go online," I say.

"Does *every* name on the list have a double consonant or a double vowel?" Rebecca asks.

"Yep. Six with consonants, four with vowels," Margaret answers. "Two with three syllables, five with two, and three with one."

"Could it be something about the characters themselves?" I ask. "Like, are they good or bad? Or their job, maybe?"

"Hmmm. Possible. But a lot of that is kind of vague," Margaret says. "For example, is Scrooge good or bad? It depends—in the beginning or at the end?"

"Why don't we just get *all* their first names and then just go around to all the pews," Rebecca suggests.

"We *could,* but somehow I don't think that would be as easy as you think. First of all, there are hundreds of pews, and second—"

Suddenly Margaret snatches the paper from my hands. "It's Copperfield!"

I look at the list to see if it will miraculously jump out at me, too. No such luck.

"Why Copperfield?" Rebecca asks.

"Because he's the only *title* character on the list. *David Copperfield*. We need to look for someone with the last name of David."

"Well, that was easy," I say.

Margaret agrees. "Almost *too* easy."

Maybe Everett Harriman wasn't all *that* after all.

Half an hour later, we are back in the church, straining our eyes in the dim light to read the worn brass plaques at the end of all the pews. There are a lot more than we expected; each pew has been donated in ten-foot sections, and each *section* has its own plaque. We start in the back and work toward the altar, pacing back and forth, back and forth. About a third of the way through, Rebecca and I shout, "Got it!" at the same time. The problem is that we are about a hundred feet apart.

" 'Gift of Anthony David,' " I say. " 'In memory of Althea David.' "

"Mine says 'Gift of Anthony David, In memory of Annabelle David,' " says Rebecca.

"Uh-oh," says Margaret. "Mine says 'Gift of Anthony David, In memory of Anne Marie David.' It was supposed to be a *single* pew, according to the clue. I'm sorry, guys. I must be wrong."

She looks so crushed.

"It's okay, Margaret," I say. "No big deal. I'm sure we'll get it."

"But I was so sure—and still wrong."

She always is. Welcome to my world, kid.

On our way back uptown, I come up with a solution. "Look, it's a literature clue. Let's just ask Mr. Eliot. He was *born* to solve this piece of the puzzle."

"But then we'll have to wait until Monday morning," Margaret says. "And besides, I want to solve it without anybody's help."

"How is using Mr. Eliot different than using the Internet?" Rebecca asks.

She has a point.

"I guess we could e-mail him," Margaret admits. Mr. Eliot *had* given us his e-mail address, which we are permitted to use for school-related communication. ("I don't want you filling up my mailbox with a bunch of stupid jokes—or worse," he said.)

"We can do better than that," I say. "I just happen to know where he lives."

Ten minutes later, we are in the lobby of Mr. Eliot's building. The doorman rings his apartment, telling him that there are three young ladies waiting downstairs and that they insist it is really important that they speak with him. Then the doorman, Freddy, as his badge indicates, listens while nodding his head before hanging up the phone without another word.

"He says he'll be down in a minute. You can wait in the lobby. You girls students of Geor—er, Mr. Eliot's?"

We all nod.

"He's a good guy, always bringing me books to read on the overnight shift."

"Lots of Charles Dickens, right?" I guess.

Freddy smiles. "No, not really. Mysteries, mostly. He loves those old 'whodunits'—Nero Wolfe, that kind of thing—but lately he's been bringing me these graphic novels. You know, the ones that look like comic books, only thicker. And with a lot more blood."

"Oooh, I love those," Rebecca says. "The gorier, the better."

"You would," I say. "You probably like all those dead teenager movies, too. All that *Nightmare on Elm Street* and *Halloween* and *I Know What You Did Last Summer* crap."

"Crap! Those are classics!"

"Prime examples of fine filmmaking," notes Margaret.

Before the conversation can sink any deeper into a discussion of who is more evil, Jason or Freddy (Krueger, not the doorman), Mr. Eliot steps out of the elevator.

"Hello, girls. Are you bothering Freddy?"

"No, no, George," says Freddy. "They're fine. We've just been having a literary discussion."

"I'll bet. Okay, what is the big crisis that has caused you to breach my sacred domicile?"

"Wait, where's your wife?" Rebecca asks. "I was hoping she'd come down, too. We want to meet her."

"She's upstairs, probably scared to death that my

students know where I live. And probably wondering, as I am, *why* they've come to my apartment building on a beautiful Sunday afternoon."

"Well, it's about the puzzle," Margaret says.

"Oh, for crying out loud. *That's* the big emergency?"

Margaret points at the tastefully decorated seating area in the lobby. "We'd better sit down, Mr. E. This may take a while."

We move to a very comfortable leather couch and chairs. Mr. Eliot listens and actually seems impressed by our resourcefulness and tenacity.

"And now you're up to the fourth clue, which is something to do with literature, and you think I can help you."

"Exact-e-ment," I say, exaggerating my French accent.

"Well, before I agree to help, tell me more about this Malcolm fellow. I just want to make sure you haven't gotten yourselves involved with some lunatic."

"Oh, I don't think he's *dangerous* or anything like that." Like I'm an expert on human nature or something. "I just think he's skeevy."

Margaret shakes her head at me. "He's *not* skeevy. Soph, you just don't like him because you think he snooped on us."

"He *did* snoop on us! And you could tell he didn't think we would ever be able to find the ring. He was like, there's no way you silly little girls from St. Veronica's are going to be able to find it without my *invaluable* help."

"He said that?"

"Well, no. But you could tell that's what he was thinking."

"So now this is about your wanting to prove him wrong. And you don't think you're all getting just a little bit *obsessed* with this story and this ring?"

"What is that line you quoted to us the first week of school?" Margaret asks. "Something some coach said? 'You've got to get obsessed and stay obsessed.' "

"Margaret, I can't believe you remember that," Mr. Eliot says. "It *was* a coach—not a real coach, but Coach Bob, a character in *The Hotel New Hampshire,* one of my all-time favorite books."

"So a little obsession is a good thing, right?" Margaret would make one heck of a lawyer.

Mr. Eliot concedes the point. "Okay, but two things before I agree to help. One, be careful. If this Malcolm guy says *anything* that sounds even the slightest bit threatening, call me, call your parents, or better, call the police. And two, when you think you've solved this thing, *please* don't just start pulling up floor tiles in the church. Father Danahey would be most displeased with you— and with me, if he knew I had anything to do with it. Promise?"

"We promise."

"All right then. We're agreed. Now tell me about this clue number four."

Margaret unfolds the clue and sets it on the coffee table before Mr. Eliot. "Which name doesn't fit?"

He picks up the paper and squints at the list of names. The lines in his forehead get deeper and deeper. He doesn't say anything for a couple of minutes, and then a slight smile creeps in. "Okay, I've got it."

A long pause.

"Well?" Rebecca says. "Tell us!"

"You really want me to just *give* you the answer? You don't want to try to figure it out on your own?"

"Just tell us, please," I say. "We promise to be good the rest of the year."

"How good? I *should* make you figure it out for yourselves. It's not that hard, really. Actually, knowing that you figured out all those other clues, I'm a little surprised you didn't get this one."

Now Margaret is miffed. "I never said we *couldn't* figure it out. I'm—we're just starting to get concerned about the time."

"Okay, okay. I didn't mean to question your abilities. Boy, you take this sleuthing stuff seriously. It's—"

Margaret holds up her hand. "Wait! Before you say it, just tell me this: who are Guppy, Summerson, and Squeers?"

"Guppy and Summerson are both from *Bleak*

House. William Guppy, I think, and Esther Summerson. And Wackford Squeers, of course, is the evil schoolmaster in *Nicholas Nickleby.* Sort of a . . . personal hero of mine."

"Did you say *Esther* Summerson?" Margaret's eyes race down the page. "The only *female.* Aaaauugghhh. I should have known that."

"Easy, Margaret," says Mr. Eliot. "You're twelve. You can't know everything. Yet."

"Trust me, she's working on it," I say. "So, you're telling me that Esther is someone's *last* name?"

"Hey, I saw that one!" Rebecca shouts. "I think I even remember where it is."

"You're not going to break into the church to look for this tonight." He looks us all in the eyes. "Promise me, girls."

"We're not going to *break* into the church," Margaret assures him. "Jeez, it's like you think we're criminals or something."

"When really we're just three innocent little schoolgirls." I bat my eyelashes for emphasis.

"Uh-huh. Seriously, ladies, stay out of trouble with this. Promise?"

"Promise."

"But . . . let me know when you find it, all right?"

Oh, yeah. He is hooked. And, later, using my trusty and well-worn nail file to remove the screws, we find a piece of paper folded perfectly to fit beneath the brass plaque that says "Gift of Dr. Ricardo Esther, In memory of Gloria Esther."

Well done! (iv) = X

You're down to the final two clues!

To find the answer for (v) use your left ear to listen very closely to the words of the dumb ox.

You know, I've got nothing against farm animals, but isn't "dumb ox" redundant? I mean, are there any *smart* ones out there?

Chapter 24

In which I learn that ice cream saves lives

Monday morning brings me back to reality. My teachers are in the midst of some kind of inhumane testing frenzy; I have an essay due in Mr. Eliot's class; and the Dickens banquet is Friday night—and so far, all we have is a script. How in the world am I ever going to find time to solve clue number five?

And then there is Leigh Ann. Who thinks Raf is cute. And nice. And funny. And available.

Deep breaths.

We meet after school in an empty room to work on our skit, which Leigh Ann finished on Sunday, adding several *pages*. Our simple five-minute skit has turned into a ten-minute playlet.

"I just thought it needed, you know, more flair, some artistic touches," Leigh Ann says as she hands out the copies.

I leaf through the pages. "Um, Leigh Ann, you realize this thing is Friday, right? This is a lot of flair and art to absorb in four days—a whole lot of flart."

"I can only stay till three o'clock," says Rebecca. "And I'm not memorizing anything. You promised."

"You don't have to memorize, Rebecca. You're just going to read a letter," Leigh Ann promises. "Guys, I've done this a million times. We can do it. C'mon, I'll show you."

Leigh Ann is a one-person production company: director, producer, actor, writer, costumer, makeup artist. She may have been selling tickets during lunch. She tells us how she has been in several plays outside of school, promises to work us like dogs to make everything *perfect*. Hell-bent on turning us into thespians, she doesn't even like the way we walk. (I wiggle. Margaret prances.) Or the way we talk. (Too fast! Too Nuuu Yawk–y!) Faster! Slower! With a little more *feeling*! Not *that* much feeling! It is maddening, and a bit terrifying, but somewhere along the line, I stop worrying about making a fool of myself and start to have fun being Master Herbert Pocket.

And then Leigh Ann's phone rings.

It is almost five o'clock, and we are starting to gather our things together to leave. I am closest to her phone when it rings, so she asks me to hand it to her. I reach for it, and in letters that burn into my retinas, the name RAF—in all caps—appears on the screen.

Stunned, and feeling the color drain from my face, I can't get rid of it fast enough. I toss it to her and go back to closing up my book bag.

Her side of the conversation goes something like this:

"Hi! . . . [*laughing*] . . . [*more laughing*] . . . At school . . . working on a skit for this banquet thing . . . Yeah, they're— . . . [*really loud laughing*] . . . I *know*! . . . Yeah, I remember . . . Really? Um, okay . . . Saturday? What time? No, I had a good time, too—"

And this is all I can take. I am hyperventilating as I run out of the room, yelling, "I've got to go!" to a very surprised and confused Margaret. I run down the hall, down five flights of stairs, and out the front doors, where I stop to take one breath before running down the sidewalk. I am halfway home when Margaret finally catches up with me, pushing me against the window of a sushi bar at Seventy-fifth and Third.

"Sophie, what is the matter with you!" She has a tight grip on my blazer as I try to wriggle away. "Didn't you hear me calling your name? And why did you just run out of the school?" Then she sees my face and stops. "Oh my gosh. Are you crying?"

"Her phone," I sniff.

"Leigh Ann's phone? What about it?"

"That was . . . Raf."

She lets go of my blazer. "How do you know?"

"I *saw* it—his name, when I gave her the phone."

"Are you sure? Why would Raf call—you don't think—"

"They're going out. I *knew* it. I am such an idiot."

"C'mon, Soph, you don't know that. It could be

totally innocent. And what about all that stuff you were just saying? How he wanted to stay and hang out with you on Saturday."

"I was wrong. C'mon, you heard her! All that laughing and talking about getting together on Saturday night," I blubber.

Margaret puts her arm around me. "I'm sorry, Soph, I really wasn't paying that much attention. I mean, I heard her laughing, but I still think you might be jumping to conclusions. Give it a little time. Come on, let's get you some ice cream."

"I'm not hungry. I just wanna go home."

"My darling friend, you don't eat ice cream because you're hungry. It's therapy that just happens to come in a bowl—with chocolate syrup and whipped cream. And frozen yogurt just isn't going to cut it. You need the real thing." She flags down a taxi, and we climb in. "We're going to Serendipity."

The driver takes a good look at my puffy red eyes as the always-prepared Margaret hands me a *much*-needed tissue. "Sometimes ya jus' gotta have some ice cream."

"You see?" Margaret says. "*Everyone* knows."

It is going to take more than two scoops of double pistachio to pull me out of my funk, though. I sit with my chin in my hands and pout while Margaret does her best to cheer me up. It just isn't *fair*. What has Leigh Ann done to deserve him? I've been his friend for *years*— helped him with homework, hung out with him after school, e-mailing, texting, everything. And what do I have to show for it?

"A really good friend?"

"I hate that."

Margaret's phone rings, reminding me to check mine for messages and that I need to call Mom and let her know I haven't been run over by a bus or something.

Suddenly Margaret is waving wildly, trying to get my attention. She mouths the words, "It's Raf," and my stomach does a double somersault. With a twist.

"I am *not* here," I whisper. I look at my phone—dead. I have forgotten to charge it again.

"Oh, I'm at home," Margaret lies. "Sophie? I don't know. So, you only call me to find out where Sophie is? Thanks a lot, Raf."

"What is he saying?" I hiss.

"Maybe she's at a movie with her mom. She probably just forgot to charge her phone. You could try her house."

What? I wave my hands back and forth. No, no, no.

"So, what's *new*?" she asks. Clever girl. "Nothing? Jeez, aren't you the one who's always telling us how much more exciting life on the West Side is?" She mouths "I tried" to me. "Are you coming to the Dickens banquet on Friday? It's going to be fun—really! We're doing a skit. Sophie, and Rebecca, and me. And Leigh Ann, you remember her? That's right. Friday, seven o'clock."

I put my hands over my ears.

When she finally snaps her phone shut, I am all over her.

"He's been trying to call *you* all day," she says. "What is up with you and that phone? I'm going to start calling you at night to remind you to plug it in."

"Nothing about . . . her?" I can't say *her* name out loud.

"Nothing. He might be just playing it cool, but if he is going out with Leigh Ann, why would he try to keep it from us? It's not like we wouldn't find out. You know, Soph, maybe if he *knew* how you felt—"

"Stop! I know. I know."

Her phone rings again.

"Oh, hi, Kate! Yeah, she's with me. She forgot to charge her phone *again*. You want to talk to her? We're on our way right now. Bye." She stands up to leave. "Your mom wants you to come home."

"You call my mom Kate?"

"Your mom is cool, and she wants me to. So, are you going to be all right?"

I feel a little better, if a little embarrassed. "Yeah. Thanks, Marg. I don't know what I would do without you."

And double pistachio ice cream.

Chapter 25

In which I go on a dream date

When I get home, I immediately plug my phone into its charger and tell Mom that if anyone calls on our main phone, I'm not home. I need to get down to some serious work on my essay about the first stage of Pip's life in *Great Expectations*. Margaret showed me her second draft during lunch, and reading it made me realize how lame my final draft was.

"This is sick, Margaret, *way* too good. You'll make the rest of us look bad if you turn in something like this." I even offered to make a few minor changes for her, to bring it down to merely dazzling. "You know, throw in a few grammatical errors, some spelling mistakes, maybe the wrong 'there' or the wrong 'your.' Mr. Eliot *loves* that. Or when you use the 'it's' *with* the apostrophe when it should be the other one. That one always gets a 'for crying out *loud*.' "

Personally, I'm not really worried about my grades; I've gotten As and Bs on pretty much everything I have done so far (except for that *una prueba horrible*). My parents expect all As, but I'm pretty sure that a B won't get me grounded or my cell phone taken away. But a C? *That* would have dire consequences.

Margaret has never received a B for a final grade. In her family, even an A-minus is a mark of slight shame, and she's concerned with her English grade. She has aced all the tests and quizzes, but Mr. Eliot gave her— and trust me, this was quite a shock to Margaret—a B-minus on a paper on Francie Nolan's coming of age in *A Tree Grows in Brooklyn,* a book Margaret absolutely loves. The fact that it was the highest grade in the class was no consolation to her, so she was pulling out all the stops, taking no prisoners, and leaving no stone unturned in pursuit of an A-plus on her *Great Expectations* paper (take your pick of clichés).

"No Bs for me," she said, gritting her teeth.

I am nearing the point where I can, with clear conscience, press "CTRL-P" and move on to other homework when he calls. I let it ring. Thirty seconds later, the house phone rings.

Mom sticks her head in my room, her hand over the phone. "Are you here for Rafael?"

I shake my head. "Tell him I'm working on an assignment that I *have* to get done."

"Why can't *you* tell him?" She pushes the phone toward me.

I back away from her like the receiver is radioactive. "Mom. Please."

She talks to Raf for a minute and then comes back and stands in my doorway. "Everything okay, Sophie?"

I play dumb. "Of course. Why?"

"You seem a little . . . are you mad at Rafael?"

I will the blood out of my face. "I'm just busy. I have a lot of homework."

"Nothing you want to talk to me about?"

"I'm fine." I open my math book and pretend to study.

"Well, when you change your mind, I'm here."

Ten minutes later, the phone rings again.

"Are you here for Margaret?"

"Yes!"

Mom grumbles something about how I'm not even a teenager yet and "it's already starting."

Margaret has just gotten off the phone with Raf. "He said he called and you wouldn't talk to him. He sounded a little sad, if that makes you feel better."

"I told my mom to tell him I was doing homework. You didn't say anything, did you?"

"No, but, Sophie, I bet he *likes* you. I've been thinking about it. The phone calls, the museum, Perkatory, your apartment—he didn't have to stick around for all that."

"Maybe. Now explain his call to Leigh Ann."

"I can't."

"So what should I do?"

"Well, this isn't exactly my area of expertise. Now, if this were, say, the early 1800s, and you were the haughty daughter of a country gentleman who was cheated out of his inheritance by his younger brother, and Raf was a dashing colonel in the British Army, just returned from service in India, *then* I'd be able to tell you exactly what to do."

"Oh, don't give me all that Jane Austen stuff. You've seen just as many cheesy teen romances as I have," I say.

That makes her laugh; she knows it is true. Margaret is not-so-secretly addicted to reruns of *Dawson's Creek*. "Officially, I have no idea what you're talking about. You've obviously confused me with one of your less stunningly sophisticated friends."

"That must be it."

"It's all going to work out, Soph."

"Don't say that! That's what parents *always* say, and it *never* works out."

We make our plans for an early-morning stop at Perkatory and then hang up. Five seconds later, the phone rings yet again. I take a deep breath and answer.

"Charge your cell phone!" Margaret shrieks. Click!

I had the strangest dream last night. Raf and I were on a date, but it was like something from the fifties. (Apparently, I really have seen *Grease* way too many times.) He was driving me home in this awesome Chevy convertible with his arm casually draped over my shoulder, the wind blowing through his hair. I couldn't take my eyes off him. One second we're going down this country road in the middle of nowhere, and then all of sudden we're at the awning outside my apartment building. He opens the car door and takes my hand, and for a few seconds, we just stand there. He is just about to kiss me when I look in the backseat of the car and see Leigh Ann. She looks up at me and smiles. *Bam!* I wake up.

Chapter 26

In which Mr. Eliot makes himself useful once again, Margaret makes herself invisible, I make a connection, and we all make a new friend

In the morning, we walk to school in a downpour of biblical proportions and arrive at Perkatory at seven, utterly soaked. Mr. Eliot is there, in his usual place with his usual coffee, *pain au chocolat,* and copy of the *Times.* He pretends to have a heart attack when he sees me. The guy's a regular riot—just ask him!

"You'll be happy to know that we were right about the clue with the names," says Margaret. "There was a Dr. Richard *Esther.* "

"The fifth clue mentions something about a dumb ox," I say, taking a huge bite of chocolate chip muffin.

"*A* dumb ox, or *the* dumb ox?"

"Ahgrowno," I mumble. Mmmm . . . *really* good muffin.

Margaret looks at the slip of paper. "It says 'use your left ear to listen *very* closely to the words of *the* dumb ox.' "

" 'Dumb ox' is somebody's nickname. Somebody important. A saint, I think. Ignatius Loyola? No, that's not it. Becket? Ask me later. I'm sure I'll remember. It's right on the tip of my tongue."

"How about Thomas Aquinas?" I ask. "You know, like the school where Raf goes."

"That's it!" Mr. Eliot practically jumps out of his seat.

"You knew all along, didn't you?" Margaret says, to which Mr. Eliot slyly grins.

"Are you serious?" I say, taking another bite of muffin. "I was right? I don't even know who he is. I was just thinking about—I mean, who is he, anyway?"

Mr. Eliot sounds like an encyclopedia entry. "Thirteenth-century Italy. Philosopher. Saint. Despite the nickname, a huge intellectual. Wrote the *Summa Theologica,* one of the most influential books of all time, basically a summary of the reasoning of the Catholic Church. Some light reading for your to-do list, Margaret."

"If he was so smart, why was he called the dumb ox?"

"When he was in school, he was bigger than the other kids and must have seemed kind of slow. There's a famous anecdote about it. Somebody said that they could call Thomas a dumb ox, but that one day his bellowing would fill the world."

A smile spreads over Margaret's brainy face. "I

know where he is. Come on, Mr. Eliot. We might need your help."

He eyes his coffee, his pastry, his paper. And then he sighs. "Oh, why not."

The church is even quieter—and darker—than usual. Other than a young (and sort of cute) priest, who at first I mistake for an altar boy, and Mr. Winterbottom, who could *never* be mistaken for a boy of any kind, we are the only people inside. Every sound we make seems amplified by the echoing emptiness. I note Mr. Winterbottom making his rounds, lighting candles and straightening the chairs on the altar for the seven-thirty Mass. He just nods and smiles at us as we pass.

The left side of St. Veronica's has a series of chapels where people can light candles or pray or just hang out near statues of their favorite saints. A statue of St. Thomas Aquinas, Mr. Not-So-Dumb Ox himself, stands in one of those chapels, cordoned off from the rest of the church by iron bars. But the thing is, there's a slight problem. Old Tom is about five feet tall and he's set into a hollowed-out space in the wall a few feet off the ground, so his head is like nine or ten feet up. We'll need a chair to reach him, but this is pew-ville, so we are going to have to improvise. The good news is once inside the chapel, we are out of sight range of our pal the security guard. And amazingly, Mr. Eliot turns out to be invaluable, as well as structurally sound. He kneels down so Margaret can use him as a stepping stool, and I help keep her steady when I'm not losing it at the sight of Margaret standing on my English teacher's back. Two questions: how *did* Professor Harriman ever place this clue, and how did he expect Caroline to get it?

"St. Pete, next time *you* get to be the stepping stool," Mr. Eliot grunts. "Okay, Margaret, now that you're up there—do you have a plan?"

"More or less," she says, struggling to maintain her balance. "Give me a second. I need to turn a little so that I can—"

"Margaret, what *are* you doing?" She has her left ear pressed against St. Thomas Aquinas's mouth and is staring straight ahead at the place where the curved wall of the niche meets the straight marble wall of the chapel.

"I think I see it. When I put my left ear against his mouth like this, like I'm listening closely to his words, my face is pointed straight ahead. I'm looking right at a narrow gap." She feels along the edge of the marble tile, her forehead creased with concentration.

"Boy, she is an intense little thing, isn't she?" whispers Mr. Eliot.

"You have no idea."

"I can hear you, you know," Margaret says, never taking her eyes off the object of her determination. "I need some tweezers. I can see it—or at least I think I can—but I can't *quite* reach it. Maybe if my fingernails were a little longer."

"Don't look at me," I say. Between the guitar and a lifelong habit of biting, my fingernails are a disaster.

"I have tweezers," says Mr. E.

He does?

He reaches into his bag—a ratty-looking green messenger bag—feels around for a few seconds, and finally pulls out a miniature Swiss Army knife. Then, to the anxiety-producing accompaniment of approaching footsteps, he hands Margaret the tiniest pair of tweezers I have ever seen—no more than an inch long. "Will these work?"

Margaret nods confidently, then waits for the footsteps to pass by. I peek out the door of the chapel and see an old woman in a babushka take a seat in a pew near the front of the church. The priest and Mr. Winterbottom are nowhere in sight. "Everything okay out there?" she asks.

"Yeah, you're good." And then, out of the corner of my eye, I see him: the cute young priest we had seen when we came in, about ten yards away and closing in fast. "Behind the statue—quick!" I hiss. "Against the wall. Hide!"

"Good morning, everyone." The priest (slightly taller than a hobbit, and nearly as cheerful) greets Mr. Eliot and me but misses seeing Margaret, who squeezes into the niche and crams herself in the best she can behind good old St. Thomas A. "Oh, I thought there were three of you."

Mr. Eliot points vaguely in the direction of the other side of the church. "Our third is around here somewhere. We're just admiring some of the artwork."

"Ah, yes, the church does have quite an impressive collection." He reaches his hand out to Mr. Eliot. "I'm Father Julian. I'm new here at St. Veronica's."

Mr. Eliot shakes his hand. "George Eliot. I teach over at the school."

"A pleasure. Can I give you a hand with anything?"

"No, thank you. We're just about done. The girls had asked about Thomas Aquinas a few days ago, and when I ran into them at the coffee shop this morning, I figured I'd bring them by for a quick look."

"Well, if you change your mind—or if you can't find your friend—let me know." With an odd smile, he turns and hobbit-walks away.

As soon as I turn around, I know what he was smiling at. Margaret's shoes, which she had taken off when she climbed up onto the ledge, are sitting right in the middle of the floor, between Mr. Eliot and me. And her feet, in her bright red socks, are ridiculously visible right next to St. Thomas's.

"Oh my God. He knew! And he didn't say anything."

"Knew what?" asks Margaret.

"Exactly where you are," Mr. E laughs.

"Are we gonna get in trouble?"

"Apparently not. I think Father Julian is, as you would say, 'way cool.' But let's not push our luck. Finish up, Margaret, and get down from there before anyone else comes in. I'd really prefer to not get arrested for such an odd violation."

Margaret goes right back to work with the tweezers, and a few moments later she holds up a folded piece of paper:

Only one more to go!

$$(v) = y$$

The answer for this clue (vi) is simple: find my father's (your great-grandfather's) portrayal of the saint with a direct connection to the item you seek.

"Oh my gosh," Margaret says. "This one really *is* too easy. Sophie, you get it too, right?" She is jumping up and down with excitement while Mr. E and I stare at the piece of paper, waiting for the answer.

He looks at me. "I'm stumped. This makes sense to you?"

"Wait a minute," I say. "Does this have anything to do with that painting that we looked at—the very first day we started looking around the church, before we even met Ms. Harriman?"

"It has *everything* to do with it." She grabs me by the arm and starts pulling. "C'mon, you guys. Other side of the church. We have to hurry; Mass starts in five minutes."

We run to the far side of the church, stopping in front of the painting that marks the sixth Station of the Cross: *Veronica Wipes the Face of Jesus.*

"This is it," Margaret says. "St. Veronica—that's her right there—was married to Zacchaeus, who is known in

France as St. *Amadour.* As in *Roc-amadour,* the town that was named for him and the town where the ring comes from. That's the connection: St. Veronica and the Rings of Rocamadour. All we have to do is look behind this painting and we will have the final piece of the puzzle."

Margaret confidently raises the same corner that Mr. Winterbottom lifted not so long ago to show us the signature on the back. "And here it is." She is rather nonchalant about it, all things considered. "Look—it's like two inches from the signature. If he had pulled it out just a little bit more, he probably would have seen it."

"And probably would have removed it," I say. "C'mon, open it up!"

Drumroll, please.

Excellent work, indeed!

$(vi) = 2$

Now that you have all six answers, you can solve the puzzle.

And by the way, happy 14th birthday!

> *With all my love and admiration on a job well done,*

> *Grandpa Ev*

Something about that last line really gets to Margaret and me. Knowing all that happened between the time that Professor Harriman wrote those words and our reading them brings us back to a certain sad reality. Finding the ring seems more important somehow— not just because it is beautiful and valuable, but because in some way it represents the lives of Caroline and her grandfather, who never got together to celebrate her success in finding it. It makes us more determined than ever to carry our mission through to the end.

We get to Mr. E's classroom and Margaret immediately starts graphing while I run down to the cafeteria to find Rebecca, who is studying for a biology test. I look around quickly—no sign of Leigh Ann. I'm okay with that. Very okay.

Rebecca and I run back up the five flights of stairs and find Mr. E watching in awe as Margaret thinks and points and plots.

She turns to face us. "Okay, are you guys ready for this? Good grief, Rebecca, are you in there? Your eyes look like they're bleeding."

Rebecca waves her off. "I was up late studying. Go ahead."

Margaret glances my way. "No Leigh Ann?"

"I looked. Didn't see her. Let's just go ahead."

"It's simple," Margaret says. "In fact, I really don't need to graph it out. I know what the solution to the system of equations is without it, but I'll do it so you can see it, too. All right, the first equation is X + 3Y = 6." She has her notebook open to the page that shows my solution. "Sophie, here's what you came up with. I'll just graph the exact same points you used."

She marks the points (3,1), (6,0), (-3,3), and (-6,4) on her graph and then carefully draws a line through all four points with a yardstick.

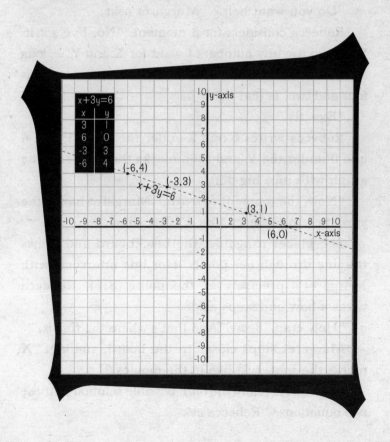

"Voilà! So much for the first equation. The second equation is $X - Y = 2$, which is even easier to figure out coordinates for. For example, if X is four, then Y has to be two, because $X - Y$ *must* equal two. Becca, I think it's your turn to solve."

Rebecca takes the chalk from Margaret and struts to the board. "Piece of cake." She starts to write something, then stops and makes a face. "Hmmm."

"Do you want help?" Margaret asks.

Rebecca considers for a moment. "No, I've got it. So, I can use any numbers I want for X and Y, as long as when I subtract them, I get two. Like, you have this four and two. Is that right?"

"Exactly."

Rebecca writes 6 and 2 under the X, and then 4 and 0 under the Y, and then marks the points on the graph with nice big dots.

"Now, the moment of truth." Margaret hands the yardstick to Rebecca like it's Excalibur.

She places it against the blackboard and draws the line through her points. Her line intersects with Margaret's precisely at the point (3,1). Rebecca takes a bow and steps aside.

"Holy crap," I say. "And that's where the ring is."

Margaret steps closer to the board, smiling. "X marks the spot. Just like in the movies."

"And this is really the *only* possible solution to those two equations?" Rebecca asks.

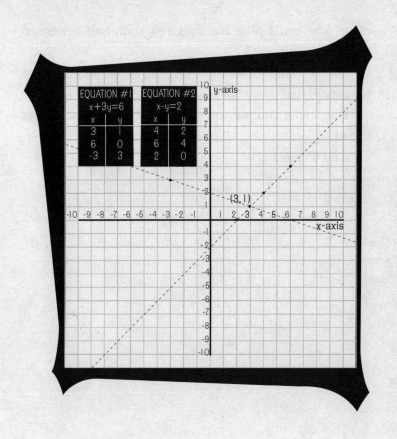

"Absolutely. Lines can only intersect at one point. It's a basic rule of geometry." Margaret is positively *glowing* with her success.

Mr. Eliot whistles in admiration. "By George, I think she's got it. Bravo, girls."

I point at Margaret. "She's way smarter than that old Nancy Drew."

"Oh, puh-leeze," Rebecca agrees. "It's not even

close. She could take Nancy Drew with half her brain tied behind her back."

"Let's wait until we have the ring in our hands before we get carried away," Margaret says.

But she is smiling, my brilliant, beautiful, amazing friend.

And so am I.

Chapter 27

Remember when Margaret said something about us being the world's worst snoops? Well, forget that she ever said it. Please.

Rebecca and I think seriously about chaining Margaret to her locker to keep her from running over to the church and starting to pull up the floor tiles right in the middle of Mass. Not that I think Father Danahey—or the dozen or so ninety-year-old women who are the early Mass regulars—would notice. Nothing slows Father Danahey down during the early Masses. Crying babies, ringing cell phones, police cars and fire trucks with sirens screaming—nothing fazes the guy. He's just a grumpy ol' Mass-sayin' machine!

Margaret finally agrees that we will have to wait until after school to get a good look at our target area—a particular location that poses a significant problem. The floor tiles are each one foot square, so if our target is the point (3,1), that means that the ring is only three feet away from a point right smack in the middle of the church. We need to figure out how we are going to lift the tile and set it back in place without showing up on the security cameras. Plus, we have to be able to do it when the church is empty, *and* without making any noise. Piece of cake, right? Cupcake? Slice o' pie?

Speaking of food, Margaret, Rebecca, and I are sitting in the cafeteria eating tacos when Leigh Ann sets her tray down. Aware that I have no right to be mad at her, I pretend to be concentrating on *Great Expectations* so I won't have to talk to her. She looks like something from the cover of *Seventeen*. Her blouse and skirt are freshly ironed, her accessories—bangles, watchband, hair clips—perfectly matched, and she is even more cheerful than usual. *Sheesh.*

"Hi, guys! Where were you this morning? I came down here before school, and nobody was here. I thought you were avoiding me," she says, laughing innocently, genuinely.

"We were up in Eliot's room," Rebecca answers. "We solved the puzzle!"

"No way! You found the ring?"

"Not yet, but we know where it is," Margaret says. "Sophie said she looked for you but you weren't around."

"I *was* a little off schedule," Leigh Ann admits. "I was up kind of late, talking on the phone."

I sneak a peek to see if she is smiling. She is. *Grrr.*

"What *happened* to you yesterday?" she asks.

I look up from my book but avoid eye contact. "To me?"

"Yeah, you just took off."

"Nothin'," I mumble. "Just had to get home." Eyes back on the page.

"Oh . . . okay. I thought maybe you guys were mad at me because of the skit. I know it's a little long, but I think it's pretty good, don't you?"

"The skit's *great,*" Margaret says.

Grrrrr squared.

Leigh Ann wanders off to the vending machines for a drink and Rebecca snatches Mr. Dickens right out of my hands. "What is your problem? I saw the way you looked at her."

"Sophie thinks that Leigh Ann—"

"Margaret! Don't. It's *nothing.*"

Now Rebecca is really interested. "C'mon, quick, before she gets back."

"Sophie likes Raf, but she thinks that he's going out with Leigh Ann, so she's mad at Leigh Ann, which really isn't fair because Sophie *told* her that Raf was available."

I pound my forehead on the table.

Rebecca swats me with my own book. "I knew it! You act like such a dork around him."

"I do not!"

"Margaret, does she or doesn't she?"

Margaret pats my arm. "Sorry, Soph. It's true. But only sometimes."

Before Leigh Ann skips back to our table, I warn

them. "I will *kill* you guys if you say anything. I mean it." And I pretend to read some more.

Miss Covergirl takes the seat next to me. "Boy, you're really into that, aren't you? I'm almost done, so I don't want to spoil it for you, but I was *really* surprised by—well, you'll see. That Miss Havisham is a nutcase. Hey—have you told Ms. Harriman about the puzzle yet?"

Margaret's face brightens. "No, but that's a *great* idea, Leigh Ann. We should go right now! We can take the inside route."

I start to say something about being late for class.

"We won't stay long," Margaret assures me. "We'll just tell her that we should have the ring by tomorrow night. She should know about this, right?"

Mere minutes later, we are past the security guard, through the locked "chalice" door (another bobby pin sacrificed for the cause), and up the scary, curvy staircase. After Margaret knocks, we hear the shuffling of papers and insistent whispering. We press our ears against the door but jerk away when we hear the CLUMP CLUMP CLUMP of heavy footsteps. As the door swings open, we are greeted by Winifred and a cloud of smoke. A cigarette dangles from her lower lip, her square face twisted into something that *resembles* a smile—or is it a glare?

"Hi, Winifred," Margaret chirps. "Is Elizabeth home?"

She mumbles and grumbles something about using

the front door like most people, then waves us in. I take a quick look around the room and notice something very peculiar: another cigarette sits in the ashtray, burning away. A thin wisp of smoke pours steadily from it, fouling the air. It is definitely not one of hers. This one is shorter and stubbier, and almost looks homemade. I try to peek behind the door, where someone might be hiding, but Winnie practically shoves me down the stairs.

She takes us down to the living room and orders us to wait. I sit in the exact spot I sat in the last time; if Winnie is going to spy on us, I'm gonna spy on her spying. Teazle jumps up next to me, taking the spot Leigh Ann has been aiming for. *Good* kitty.

Ms. Harriman practically bursts into the room. She's wearing a bright red blazer—just like ours, sans crest. "Girls! It is so good of you to come and see me." She shakes each of our hands and holds on for several seconds. She has a strange way of looking me right in the eyes, almost as if she's trying to read my mind. To be honest, it makes me a little squirmy.

After handshakes, she starts right in with the "lightning round" questions (and answers). "How are you all? You look wonderful. I *do* love those blazers. After you were here the last time, I went right out to Bloomie's and bought one for myself." She twirls in the center of the room, showing it off. "Oh, let's not talk about me. Tell me about you. Tell me everything. Oh my goodness, would you like some tea? We must have tea. Winnie!

Would you make us some tea, please? And bring out a plate of cookies. Now, where were we? Rebecca, I'm so glad you came Saturday. You must tell me all about your lessons, after you get started, of course. Sophie, how is your guitar playing coming along? I think it's just wonderful that you take your music so seriously. And, Margaret, I hear you're a wonderful violinist."

Many minutes and dozens of questions later, Winnie brings in the tray with the tea and cookies, creating just enough of an interruption that Margaret finally has a chance to convey our reason for stopping by.

"Elizabeth, we have some very good news," Margaret announces, taking a cookie from the plate.

"How exciting!"

"We know where the ring is, and if everything goes according to plan, we will have it tomorrow."

"Oh! Of course! The puzzle! *That's* why you're here!"

For crying out loud! Why *else* would we be here? I shoot a quick glance at Margaret, but she just smiles. Wait. Did I just say "for crying out loud"?

"Girls, this is absolutely incredible! I wasn't expecting anything for weeks and weeks. Tell me how it happened." She is literally on the edge of her seat.

Margaret recites the slightly abridged version of the story (leaving out all of the math, thank God). I watch and listen while Winnie refills our teacups and passes the cookie plate around. She leaves the room, but I spot her snooping in her usual spot. What is *up* with her? I am keeping a pretty close eye on her in the mirror when I realize she is watching me. So, if I have this straight, I'm watching her watching me watching her watch everyone else. Oy. We are both a little surprised that we've been caught, and for a moment we just stare uncomfortably at each other. The next time I check the mirror, I can't see her, but I'm *sure* she's still listening.

When Margaret finishes the story, Ms. Harriman sits back in her chair, shaking her head slowly with a rueful smile. "You accomplished it all so quickly. Even if the ring isn't there, you girls have done more for me than you can imagine. You see, I have just made a very important decision, and I owe it all to you. I need to see my daughter. It's time for my family's foolishness to end, and it's up to me to end it."

"Oh, that's wonderful," Leigh Ann says. "I'm sure she will be so happy. Everybody needs their mom."

"How do you think you'll do it? I mean, will you just call her up, or . . ." I mean, just how *do* you make up with someone you stopped talking to?

"Well, I suppose I'll just have to swallow my pride and ask Malcolm for his help."

"Why don't you ask her to come to the Dickens banquet on Thursday?" Leigh Ann suggests. "It's going to be lots of fun. Our English teacher is in charge. He dresses up like Charles Dickens and people wear top hats. You could watch the skits, and there's a dinner, too."

"Goodness. That does sound interesting."

"I don't know, Leigh Ann," Rebecca says. "They haven't seen each other in a long time. Maybe they want something a little more . . . private."

"No, no, I think I like this idea. We'll have to talk on the phone first, but I think this banquet Leigh Ann described is the perfect place to meet in person—if she'll come."

Leigh Ann claps her hands. "Yay! I'll stick a flyer in the mail slot in your door this afternoon. It has all the information. This is so exciting!"

"Do you really think you'll come?" Margaret asks.

"I wouldn't miss it for the world. I just hope my *daughter* will be accompanying me." She gets a little misty. "I can't tell you how nice it is to say those words."

Later that afternoon, Margaret and I are standing on Lexington Avenue, staring up at St. Veronica's Church.

"Ready?"

"Set!"

"Let's go."

We could hear the organ from the street, and inside we can *feel* it; the organist is seriously rockin' the joint.

"Bach," Margaret says. "Cool."

"Sounds like a haunted house. Or *The Phantom of the Opera.*"

Robert is nowhere in sight, but the September issue of *Elle* is open on his desk ("Hate Him? Date Him!").

We push through the swinging glass doors and into the nave.

"Gone for the day," I say. "Maybe the organist locks up when he leaves."

"Hope so."

We sneak along the side aisle, past the paintings where we had found the first and last thumbtacked clues, and make our way up to the edge of the raised section of the floor. Starting from the intersection of the two metal strips that was the zero point on our graph, Margaret counts the tiles to find the one where the point (3,1) is located.

"Uh-oh."

"What do you mean, uh-oh?" I hiss.

"It's under the table."

The altar table is about seven feet long and three feet wide, and it straddles the tile we need to get to. A tailored satin cloth covers it completely, hanging nearly to the floor on all four sides.

"What do we do?" I ask.

"This table weighs a ton. The wood on the top is like two feet thick. There's no way we can move it."

She looks around the church to see if anyone is watching, but it appears to be deserted, except for the organist, who is up in the loft and facing away from us. I can just barely see the top of his head.

"Well, let's go have a look."

Margaret crosses herself, steps up onto the worn

stone floor, and silently ducks down under the table, behind the tablecloth. I do the same, after taking one last
quick look around the church.

"We're in," I say, as if we have just broken through
a sophisticated security system and are about to save the
world by disarming some nuclear missiles.

"Okay, this is the spot. The good news is that the tiles
don't seem to have any cement around them. They
ought to be easy to lift up."

"Them? They?"

"Oh yeah, I guess I forgot to mention that part. You
see, I really don't know which *exact* tile it is."

"WHAT!"

"Oh, relax. Jeez, you talk about *me* spontaneously
combusting. Look, the actual intersection is really *between* the tiles, right? So we might have to lift all four."

"So what's the problem?"

"This table leg is sitting right smack in the middle of
the intersection of the four tiles."

"So what does that mean?"

"Here, try to lift it up."

We both reach under the edge of the tabletop—and
heave!

Yikes. "I think I strained something. This is like
something out of a freaking castle."

Margaret shushes me. "Someone's coming. Under the
table. I heard a door open, over by the dressing room."

The music stops abruptly, and the sound of footsteps

suddenly becomes clear and is getting closer. My heart begins jackhammering into my rib cage and when the tip of a man's black shoe appears under the edge of the tablecloth, I seriously think I might puke.

Black Shoe Man stands at the table for the world's longest minute. Will Robert's hearing aid pick up the sound of my beating heart? Margaret makes the "deep breath" sign with her hands.

The damn shoes finally move a few steps away, but they stop again near the podium on the left side of the altar. From under the tablecloth, we can't see anything above ankle height.

"He's kneeling down," I whisper, mere inches from Margaret's ear. "He's looking for something."

"Who is it?"

"I can't tell." The organist launches into another raucous passage of Bach, allowing me the chance to shift positions and take another deep breath without fear of being heard. Something in my book bag is digging into my back, so I carefully slip it off my shoulders. By the time things quiet down again, Margaret indicates that the visitor has moved to the other side of the table, nearer to me.

"Can you see him now?" she whispers.

I gently shift so I can look, and—yipes!—he is standing right beside me. A few seconds later, I see his feet go through the side door into the dressing room and then the door shuts behind him.

"He's gone," I say, taking a much-needed breath.

"Good. I don't know how much longer I could have taken it."

"I was *dying*."

"That's what I mean. I don't know how much longer I would have been able to stand watching you. You look so terrible."

"Hey, thanks. So, can we get out of here now?"

"Let's be sure he's really gone first."

When Margaret signals, we slide out from under the table and hurry off the altar to the aisle opposite where the black shoes had disappeared. We turn the corner . . . and practically knock over St. Veronica's half-blind, hard-of-hearing, fashion-magazine-reading security guard.

"Oh, hello, Robert."

Chapter 28

Can you imagine? Margaret and me, suspects in a crime?

"Hold it right there, girls."

We are *seriously* busted.

"What were you girls doing up there?"

"What?" When in doubt, act stupid.

"I saw you come out from under the altar table."

"We weren't *doing* anything," Margaret says. "Really. Don't you remember us? We were here a few days ago, working on a project. We go to school next door. Here's my ID. We were just looking around, taking some more pictures, because it's due tomorrow, and we forgot part of it. Swear to—"

The security guard looks skeptical. "We've had some trouble. I'm supposed to take anything suspicious over to Father Danahey."

"Suspicious! Oh, come on. We're just students." Apparently, Margaret's strategy is to play the "mischievous but innocent schoolgirl."

2 I 3

Robert calls up to the organist to let him know that he will be back in a few minutes. "C'mon, young ladies. Let's go."

And so, here we sit, the picture of guilty innocence, awaiting our fate on a bench in the pastor's office.

Father Danahey barges into the office. He's about six foot three, with hair like a paintbrush, all gruff and no-nonsense. Margaret and I start to stand when he barks, "Sit. First, your names."

We introduce ourselves, adding quickly that we both go to school at St. Veronica's in the hope that this piece of information will automatically absolve us.

But: not so much.

"Robert tells me that you were *under* the altar table. Is that right?"

"Well, yes," Margaret says. "But we—"

"And that you were *running* out of the church when he found you."

"Yes, Father," she admits.

Father Danahey looks first at Margaret, then at me, and turns his palms upward. His bushy eyebrows move in the same direction.

My palms are sweating, and my stomach is starting to hurt.

"But see, we weren't doing anything bad," Margaret begins. "We're working on a project, and we needed to look at a few more things in the church. I know, we shouldn't have been up on the altar, but Mr. Winter-bottom let us go up there before to take pictures of the stained glass. And then, when we heard someone com-ing, we just panicked and hid."

"And that's the whole story, eh?" Father Danahey leans back in his chair. He looks tired, too tired to be dealing with teenage girls. "You must admit, it sounds a little fishy."

"I do admit that," Margaret says as I begin to envi-sion the two of us breaking rocks in those *very* unflat-tering prison jumpsuits.

"You see, girls, I want to believe you. I'm still not en-tirely convinced by your explanation, but I also don't think you intended to do anything wrong. Of course, you might be pulling the wool over these old Irish eyes. You see, a few days ago, a small statue of St. Andrew disap-peared from one of the old corridors, and sometime in the last twenty-four hours, someone walked off with two candlesticks that were sitting right on top of the table where you just happened to be hiding. Now, ordinarily, that wouldn't be such a big deal, because candlesticks can be replaced. But these were special. They may not have looked like much, but I'm told that when it comes to the value of antiques, that doesn't mean a thing. For example, that monstrosity of a table you were hiding un-der. It was made sometime in the Middle Ages for a cas-tle in Scotland, and they tell me it's worth a small fortune. The candlesticks came from the same castle, and they also date back to the Middle Ages. As a matter of fact, I was just meeting with a parishioner about them; he's an expert on such artifacts and I asked him to come in and tell me about them—their potential value and so forth. Now do you see my problem?"

Margaret is indignant. "You think *we* stole them? I've never stolen anything in my life, and it was just that *one* time when Sophie—"

Deafening, terrifying, I-think-my-jaw-just-hit-the-floor silence.

Margaret knows from the look on Father Danahey's face that she's already said too much, and her hand flies up to cover her mouth.

She tries to recover, but the damage is done. "But that was *years* ago!"

"Exactly *what* was years ago?" Father Danahey glares at me across the table. Gulp.

Here's an unembellished, honest-to-God true confession: I, Sophie St. Pierre, have a criminal past.

"But wait," says Margaret, now in tears. "You can't . . . she would never . . . oh my gosh, Sophie, I am so sorry. Please, Father Danahey, you have to believe me. It wasn't her fault. It was *nothing*."

"Miss St. Pierre, why don't you tell me about this *other* time and let me decide. There are tissues on the table behind you, Miss Wrobel."

Surprisingly, I'm not that nervous as I tell him the story. "We were in the fourth grade. It was the last day of school before Christmas vacation and our class went to St. Patrick's Cathedral for a special Mass and then to the gift shop next door."

"You stole from the gift shop at St. Patrick's?"

I nod. "But it's not as bad as it sounds, really. I was kind of a . . . victim of circumstances. See, my dad is from France, and we were flying to Paris that night. I was a little nervous about the trip, and in the store there's this beautiful St. Christopher medal that I really wanted, because I had just learned about him being the patron saint of travelers and all that. It was like five dollars, and I only had three dollars with me. And that's when this *other* girl gets involved."

"Bridget O'Malley," sniffs Margaret.

"She starts telling me these stories about the *Titanic* and all these plane crashes, and how the only people who survived were the ones wearing their St. Christopher medals, and that if I didn't have one, well, you know. And I believe her because, I mean, I'm nine years old and getting on a plane in a few hours, and by that point, I'm scared to death. So I took it—but I *swear* to you that I was going to come back and pay for it when I got back from France. I swear."

"But you got caught."

I nod again. "Red-handed. By Sister Antonia—she runs the place. And for three months, I had to go help out her and the other sisters in the store on Saturdays, and my parents grounded me and made me go to confession. *And* I swore I would never steal anything for the rest of my life. And I haven't. And I won't."

Father Danahey rubs his forehead, eyes closed. "Hmmm."

I am trying to decide if that was a "Hmmm—sounds believable" or a "Hmmm—that's a really lame story" when someone comes up behind us and clears his throat.

Father Danahey waves at him. "Malcolm, do come in. Girls, this is Dr. Chance. He is sort of our, um, unofficial church historian."

I spin around to see that tweedy, creepy Malcolm Chance, looking even tweepier than usual.

"Ah, we meet again. Good evening, girls."

"You know each other? Maybe I should get Gordon in here as well." Father Danahey steps out into the hallway and shouts, "Gordon! Can you come in here, please?" Then, turning back to Malcolm, he says, "So, you *do* know these girls?"

"Oh, yes. These young ladies are friends of Elizabeth's. We share some . . . common interests, you might say."

"You don't say. Common interests like the Yankees, or common interests like medieval religious antiquities?"

"The latter, I'm afraid."

"Interesting." Father Danahey waves another man into the cramped office. "Gordon, thanks for coming. Girls, this is our deacon, Mr. Winterbottom."

Even if I were blind, I would still know Mr.

Winterbottom was in the room. The guy's an ashtray with legs.

Father Danahey continues. "I was just telling the girls about our missing candlesticks. They assure me that they had nothing whatsoever to do with that unfortunate incident. They also mentioned that you had let them take some pictures behind the altar. Does that ring any bells?"

Mr. Winterbottom's yellow eyes dart back and forth from Margaret to me. "Yes, as a matter of fact, I did help them out once or twice. They seemed especially interested in some of the artwork and the Nativity figures."

Well, *that* was helpful. Thanks for throwing us under the bus, Mr. Winterbutt.

Just then, Father Julian, dressed in a sweat suit and running shoes and sweating profusely from his forehead, appears in the doorway. He recognizes me immediately and seems utterly confused by our presence in Father Danahey's office.

"Evening, Father, Dr. Chance. Girls? What's going on?"

"Well, everyone seems to know you two except me," Father Danahey says.

Father Julian smiles, and I know that we have at least one ally in the room. He points directly at me. "Well, I know *this* one. I met her, along with one of her teachers, in the church this morning. I believe they were doing some research."

"So you've actually seen her working on this project?"

"Oh, yes."

"And you'll vouch for her?"

"Definitely."

"And what about you?" Father Danahey looks straight at Margaret.

Father Julian winks at me. "I don't know. She looks like a shady character to me," he says, smiling broadly.

"That's good enough for me, then." Father Danahey fights back a smile of his own. "Young ladies, we won't say anything to your parents about this—yet. But, girls, go *home*. And no future sneaking about the church, understand?"

"Yes, Fa-ther Dan-a-hey," we say dutifully. As I stand up to leave, I push the hair out of my eyes and notice Mr. Winterbottom focusing on the second finger of my right hand, where I wear a single ring, turned so that only the gold band is visible.

"That's an interesting ring," he lies. "Do you mind?"

"What, this?" I turn the ring so he can see the stone. It is an authentic seventies "mood ring" that I picked up for four bucks in a vintage clothing shop in the Village.

"Hey, I remember those," Father Julian says. "A mood ring, right? Boy, I haven't seen one in years. What does that color mean?"

The stone is coal black. "I think it means that I need some coffee-toffee ice cream. With sprinkles."

He gets a chuckle out of that. "I'll show you girls out."

Margaret turns back to Father Danahey and Malcolm one last time. "We really are sorry, Father. We won't do it again. We promise."

"Good night, Miss Wrobel. Remember, straight home."

Father Julian leads us out to the rectory entrance and opens the door.

"I think you saved our lives in there," I say.

"Oh, I don't think the Church burns very many people at the stake these days—at least not for minor offenses. But one day I'd like to hear what is *really* going on, okay?" Pretty smart for a hobbit.

Chapter 29

In which I learn so much more than I need to know about men's shoes

We start to go straight home, both a little too freaked out to talk much. I mean, what with being minor suspects in a heist and Margaret dredging up my shameful past at the worst possible moment and all. About two blocks from the church, it hits me like a piano falling from a ten-story building. "MY BAG! Oh my God. I don't have my bag!"

"Are you sure you had it with you when we left school today?"

"Positive! Remember, I took my phone out of it before we went into the church." I reach into my coat pocket and pull out the phone.

"So, you must have left it in Father Danahey's office. I'm sure you can get it from him tomorrow morning."

I rack my brain, trying to remember where I left it. "No, no, see, I didn't have it with me in his office."

"Are you sure?"

And then the second piano hits me. "Oh, no."

" 'Oh, no' what?" Suddenly Margaret looks worried.

"I didn't have it with me in the waiting room."

It only takes her a second to realize what that means. "Gulp. You left it somewhere in the church?"

"Under the table. When we were hiding there, something in the bag was digging into my back, so I took it off when the music was really loud."

Margaret starts laughing like a lunatic. "Sophie, you are the worst criminal ever. Never mind fingerprints, officers, here's my book bag with everything you'll need to identify me."

"It's not funny. What am I going to do? How am I going to get it back? And what am I supposed to do tonight? My books are in there, I have homework I gotta do. And our skit—you know I need to work on my lines."

"All true, but there's no way we can retrieve it tonight. You can use my books to study. In the morning, we tell the security guard some version of what happened and he'll get it for you."

My heart rate returns to normal, and we turn and go down the stairs to the subway stop at Sixty-eighth Street.

"Hey, did you notice their shoes?" Margaret asks as we swipe our cards and pass through the subway turnstiles.

"Whose shoes?"

"All the men in Father Danahey's office."

Shoes? I was too busy watching the DVD of my life pass before my eyes—a decidedly G-rated piece of film-making, I'm sorry to report.

"Well, I'm going to bet you remember *the* shoes, the ones that practically kicked us when we were under the table. What did they look like?"

"I don't know. Black penny loafers. Ordinary. Men's shoes."

"That's right. Did you notice the security guard's? His were more like sneakers."

"So that means it wasn't him up there on the altar when we were. Maybe it was Father Julian."

"Nope. Remember, he was wearing running clothes with sneakers."

"Which leaves—"

"Father Danahey was wearing brown shoes. Hush Puppies."

"Malcolm!"

"Bingo. Kinda."

"Meaning?"

"He was wearing black penny loafers, slightly worn. But here's the thing—Winterbottom was wearing them, too."

Why was I disappointed?

"But if it was Malcolm—what was he doing?"

"Same thing we were. Doesn't it seem like a pretty weird coincidence that he was kneeling down on the floor looking for something not five feet away from where *we* were looking?"

"But how could he know where to look? We figured out all those riddles, and there was only one note and one set of clues. Do you think he was spying on us the whole time?"

"Or maybe he had someone doing it *for* him," Margaret says. "Like Elizabeth's housekeeper, Winifred."

"She's in cahoots with him. I *knew* there was something strange about her."

"Sophie, you think there's something strange about everyone."

"Well, this time I'm right. So what do we do?"

"Actually . . . I have no idea."

Hmmm. Margaret without an idea. Now that's a first.

"So what do you think about those missing candlesticks? Malcolm, too?"

"Could be, but why?"

"Oh, come on, Soph. For the money, of course. Father Danahey said that they didn't look like much. Malcolm's probably one of the few people around who would have any idea what they were worth. And because he's a trusted, upstanding member of the parish, he can pretty much do as he pleases in the church. It's like he has a backstage pass."

And so the race is on: the Red Blazer Girls versus Malcolm and Winnie, the Bonnie and Clyde of the Upper East Side.

Chapter 30

In which my life is turned upside-down, topsy-turvy, helter-skelter, and torn asunder

In the morning, I am wide awake *before* my mom calls for me, for the first time in my life, I am reasonably certain. It is Thursday, and I have a full day ahead of me, and possibly a nervous breakdown. Even though Mom has a busy day of her own, she still makes me blueberry pancakes. All right! I thank her as I run out the door, reminding her that it is dress rehearsal day for the Dickens banquet and I'll probably be pretty late.

When Margaret and I get to the church, several trucks are parked outside, and the sidewalk is bustling with workers carrying scaffolding and other heavy equipment inside. The renovations are officially under way, and the odds of success in Project: Ring Retrieval are sinking by the minute.

Robert is at the security desk, immersed in *Marie Claire*.

"Does he ever go home?" I whisper unnecessarily.

"Morning, ladies. Got something for one of you."

"Oh, good, you found it."

Robert stares blankly at me. "Found it? Didn't find anything. This is from Mr. Winterbottom. For a . . . Sophie St. Pierre. That you?"

"Yes, that's me," I say, utterly baffled. "But what about my bag?"

"Don't know nuthin' about a bag. Was told to give you this when you showed up, so here you go."

I open the envelope. Inside is a note, printed in large, blocky letters.

I HAVE YOUR BAG.
WE NEED TO TALK.
JUST YOU AND ME.
COME TO THE RECTORY
AS SOON AS YOU
FINISH READING THIS.

That's it?

Margaret reads it, frowning. "Why didn't he just leave the bag here?"

"Did he happen to say anything about what he wanted?" I ask.

"Nope. Handed me the envelope and told me to give it to you as soon as you got here. Said you'd be in early." He turns back to "Ten Things He'll Never Tell You About His Past!"

Margaret peers through the doors that separate the

227

foyer from the nave of the church. Construction workers are setting up ladders, portable lights, and other equipment, and covering the pews on the left side of the church with acres of drop cloths.

The security guard shakes his head. "Can't let you inside, girls. We'll only be open for a few hours today, two o'clock to five o'clock. They're going to be doing some work on the ceiling. Only the chapel down the hall here is open."

"I don't care what the letter says; I'm going with you," asserts Margaret. We march out the door and up the stairs to the rectory, where we pause to collect ourselves.

"Maybe he just wants to warn me about Malcolm." I press the buzzer.

A few seconds later, Mr. Winterbottom's unnaturally tanned face appears behind the door. He opens it partway and says, "Which one of you is St. Pierre?"

"That's me."

"Just you."

"Can't I wait inside?" Margaret says. "It's cold out here."

He opens the door and lets us in, directing Margaret to the room where we had waited for Father Danahey and motioning for me to follow him to his office.

"Now then," he says, lighting a cigarette with shaking hands. "Let's get right down to brass tacks. We each have something that the other wants. I have your bag, and you—well, you have something very special."

"Look, Mr. Winterbottom, I swear I didn't take those candlesticks, if that's what you're talking about."

"We'll get to those in a minute. I'm much more interested in some information that you have and that I need."

"Are you sure you have the right girl?"

"Quite sure. Sophie St. Pierre. Lovely name, by the way."

"What kind of information?"

"Don't be coy." He taps his ashes into an overflowing ashtray. "It concerns the whereabouts of a certain valuable item—a religious relic. One that has been hidden in the church for a long time—twenty years, to be precise."

Jeez. How does *he* know this? "Look, I'm not admitting anything, but even if I knew anything about this thing you're talking about, why would I tell *you* about it? What's in it for me? I get my bag back? Big deal. I'm willing to take a chance that I can get new books and that L.L.Bean has a few more backpacks just like that one."

Mr. Winterbottom takes a long puff from his cigarette and stares right back at me, with his version of a smirkle slowly pulling half of his mouth upward. Then he theatrically sets the cigarette in the ashtray and applauds me. "Bravo. Outstanding performance, Miss St. Pierre, truly. Really, I do admire your—dare I say it—your chutzpah, but it's not quite as simple as you think. You see, there is the matter of the candlesticks."

"What about them? We already told Father Danahey we didn't have anything to do with them. And he believed us." And that's when I notice his cigarettes. Short and stubby, homemade-looking things. Just like the one I'd seen burning in the ashtray at Ms. Harriman's.

"Then perhaps you would like to explain what they are doing in your backpack, which I discovered under the altar table—not five feet from where they disappeared." He reaches under his desk and pulls out my bag, unzipping it just enough to reveal the tops of two wooden candlesticks.

"Hey, wait a minute." I stand up, protesting. "That's not—"

"*Fair*? Is that what you were going to say? Look, I'm going to make this real simple. You have twenty-four hours. Tomorrow morning at seven o'clock sharp, you are going to meet me at the church, alone. We will have half an hour before the workers start; you're going to retrieve this item for me and then we're going to make a little trade. If you don't show up, I take the bag to Father Danahey, and thanks to your little friend's embarrassing disclosure of your past—well, I'm sure you can guess the rest. And oh, I almost forgot to mention the missing statue of St. Andrew—the very one you seemed so interested in the other day. I wonder when that will turn up."

Oh, he is good.

"One question. What makes you so sure that we know where the, uh, this thing is?" I know the answer, of course; I just want to see if he'll admit it. Winnie has been spying for *him* all along, not Malcolm. But why— what is the connection between those two?

Unlike all those crooks on TV who always explain everything, though, he simply escorts me out to the front door, where Margaret stands waiting.

"Is everything all right? You look a little pale. And where's your bag?"

"Oh, she'll be fine. She just needs a little fresh air." He blows some smoke our way for emphasis. "Good day, girls. I'll be seeing you soon. *Very* soon. Toodle-oo."

Outside, Margaret takes me by the arm and leads me down the steps and around the corner to Perkatory. She doesn't say anything until we sit down.

"Okay, spill it!"

"I'm so sorry, Margaret." I fight back tears and can't look her in the eyes.

She takes my hand. "Sophie St. Pierre, what are you talking about? What happened in there?"

"It was *him* in the church last night, not Malcolm. He knows about the ring. Winnie has been spying for him. He says that I have to help him find it at seven o'clock tomorrow morning, or he'll take my bag to Father

Danahey. And guess what ended up in my bag? Those missing candlesticks. And the missing statue that Father Danahey mentioned? It just happens to be the one I asked Winterbottom about while you were looking at the Christmas stuff. He's gonna say that he found the bag under the table, and they were all in it."

"And you think Father Danahey's going to believe that you stole those things?"

"Admit it, Margaret, it looks pretty bad. My word against the word of the church deacon. Who would *you* believe? And now that Danahey knows about my, um, past, if Winterbottom takes him that bag, I'm toast."

"Then we're a pair of . . . toast. We're in this together, Sophie, especially since it's my own stupid fault that anyone even knows about that silly St. Christopher medal. But there's no way we're handing that ring over to that sleazeball. There has to be another way. You know, I can't believe he turned out to be so . . . scummy. Don't you think it might be best to go straight to Father Danahey, like right now, and tell him what happened? How would Winterbottom explain your meeting?"

"Father Danahey's not there today. I overheard him last night talking to Father Julian. He's going to Pittsburgh or someplace to see his sister. He'll be gone until Monday."

"Hmmm. I have to think." She puts her hands over her ears, and a minute passes. Finally, she speaks. "We'll just have to get the ring out of there *today*."

I shake my head. "Impossible. Winterbottom, the security guard, the construction workers, Malcolm, Father Julian, and all the other priests. There is no way we can go in there without getting caught."

"Nothing is impossible. We need some help—and I think I know just the person to ask."

It is all I can do to keep from laying my head on the table and sobbing. "Who?"

"Malcolm Chance."

I stare at her. "An hour ago you thought he was the enemy."

"I was wrong. He can help us. Remember, he has the 'backstage pass' to the church."

"I'm sure he *could* help us, but why *would* he?"

"Well, for one thing, I'm pretty sure that he wouldn't want Mr. Winterbottom to have the ring any more than we do."

Good point. "But how is Malcolm ending up with the ring any better than Winterbottom? Isn't one just as bad as the other?"

"It's entirely possible that we have misjudged Malcolm. Think about it. Has he really ever done anything to us? Sure, his ex-wife doesn't care much for him, but how many people out there go around saying nice things about their exes? Don't get me wrong; I like Elizabeth, but she *is* a bit batty."

Margaret's plan to join forces with Malcolm has another element: we can play the "family card." Her theory is that the ring truly belongs not to him, not to Ms. Harriman, but to Caroline, their daughter. After all, it *was* her birthday present.

I have my doubts about the plan, but I know I only have two choices: make nice to Malcolm or pack my bag for juvie hall.

Chapter 31

In which my day grows curiouser and curiouser and . . . I withhold a teensy-weensy piece of information

And so my fate lies in the hands of the unlikely duo of Margaret Wrobel and Malcolm Chance. First, we go online in the library and find his office number at Columbia. Margaret leaves him a message to call her cell phone, and we cross our fingers and head back down to the cafeteria.

Leigh Ann, her perky little self, is studying for a vocabulary quiz with Rebecca. I spin around and try to head back upstairs to our locker, but Margaret won't let me.

"I know it's rude," I admit, "but I already have too much on my mind to deal with *her.*"

"Soph, we're going to need her help tonight, so you're going to *have* to deal. Let's just get through this ordeal and the banquet Friday night, then we'll figure it all out."

I plonk myself down on the chair and sigh deeply.

Rebecca yanks her thumb at me. "What's *her* problem?"

"You okay, Sophie?" asks Leigh Ann.

Why does she always have to be so damn nice?

"She's had a rough twenty-four hours," Margaret says. "We kind of got busted in the church last night, and now her book bag is being held for ransom."

"What?!"

When Margaret gets to the end of our whole sordid tale, Rebecca says, "Man, you guys are my heroes. What are you gonna do?"

"What *we're* going to do," says Margaret, "is get the ring *tonight,* assuming that we get Malcolm to help."

"How do you know this Malcolm guy's not going to scam you?" Rebecca says.

"Look, Sophie's future is at stake here, and I made things worse when I opened my *grande bouche* about that stupid St. Christopher medal. So either we get Malcolm to help or we break in after hours without him. If we got caught doing that—"

Leigh Ann whistles. "We'd be expelled for sure."

"You guys *are* coming with us tonight," says Margaret, very matter-of-factly. "That table weighs a ton. Before you say anything, Rebecca, I will talk to your mom."

"What! No way."

"I'm serious. I'll tell her the truth—that we're helping out a woman in the parish."

"And what are you gonna say we're doing for this lady?"

"That we're helping her . . . look for something important. C'mon, Rebecca, trust me. It'll work."

"Look, I know you're Miss Goody Two-shoes and all, but my mom doesn't know that. I just . . . oh, fine! I'll come!"

Behold the power of peer pressure.

Margaret's phone rings in the middle of Mr. Eliot's class, just after he asks me to describe some of the changes Pip undergoes during his first few months in London. She lunges for it, knocking her books off the desk in the process.

"My, isn't *this* an interesting development? You know, Miss Wrobel, I'm under strict orders from Sister Bernadette to confiscate cell phones that are used during school hours." He holds out his palm.

Margaret sets her phone in his hand. "I'm *so* sorry, Mr. Eliot. I forgot that it was on. *Please* don't take it to the office. It will never happen again."

"I'll tell you what. If Miss St. Pierre answers the question to my satisfaction, you get the phone back. If she blows it, it's mine."

I immediately start spouting everything I can think of. "Pip turns into an irresponsible jerk. He spends all his money, and he is always going to Jaggers for more. And on top of that, he is becoming a snob. I mean, the way he treats poor Joe when he comes to visit—"

Mr. Eliot holds up his hand to stop me and hands the phone back to Margaret.

"Very nice, Miss St. Pierre. I notice that you don't have your books with you today. I trust that is also a one-time-only event."

Margaret turns to thank me and mouths the words "That was Malcolm."

When the bell rings, we rush into the bathroom to listen to his message. He was "a bit surprised" to hear from us, and "more than a little curious," and he agreed to meet us at Perkatory at four-thirty. *And* he promised not to mention it to *anyone,* a condition Margaret had insisted upon.

"You still think we can trust him?" I ask.

Margaret puts her arm around me. "As far as I can throw him."

At two-thirty, Margaret and I are on our way up to Mr. Eliot's classroom on the fifth floor to meet Leigh Ann for skit practice when the principal, Sister Bernadette, looking highly, um, unpleased, intercepts us.

"Just the two I'm looking for." She places a hand on each of our shoulders. "Come with me."

We march up the stairs and into her office. What now?

"Sit," she commands, as if we are cocker spaniels. "I'll be right back."

Sister Bernadette has a tough-but-fair reputation. She isn't one of those "wrath of God" nuns, but she isn't exactly the Mother Teresa type, either.

I look to Margaret. "You think Father Danahey told her?"

"Shhh. Here she comes."

Sister Bernadette strides into the room, and rather than sitting behind her desk, she sets a third chair right in front of us and sits down. "Ladies, I just had a rather interesting conversation with Father Danahey, who called me from somewhere in Pennsylvania, of all places. Ah, Mr. Eliot. Join us. Thank you for coming. Here, take this seat." She yields her chair to him and moves behind her desk.

"Hello, girls. Sister."

"Hi, Mis-ter El-i-ot." We are *so* obviously trying to act cheerful and sickeningly innocent.

"Father Danahey has just informed me that the night security guard in the church caught these two coming out from under the table on the altar."

"He *what*?"

We attempt to shrink ourselves down to microscopic size, but they can still see us. Sister Bernadette goes on with the distasteful tale.

"It was last evening. They *claim* to have been working on a 'project' "—Sister Bernadette even uses air quotes when she says it!—"for their religion class. I have yet to check with their teacher about the existence of this mysterious project that allegedly has them crawling around the altar floor at all hours like church mice."

Yipes. I look at Mr. Eliot, my eyes begging him not

239

to betray us before we figure out how to weasel our way out of this one.

"You were *under* the table on the altar? Why?"

"We were hiding," I say.

"From some guy who was sneaking around the church," adds Margaret. "We were just looking around, not hurting anything, and suddenly there was this guy there. We got scared and hid under the table."

Sister Bernadette scoffs. "What 'guy'? And why did you feel the need to hide from him?"

Hmmm. A reasonable question. So, what would be a reasonable answer?

"Well, we knew that we weren't supposed to be in there, and when we heard him, we thought at first that it was the security guard. We didn't want to get into trouble," Margaret explains.

Mr. Eliot leans in. "But it wasn't the security guard?"

"No. The man went into the dressing room at the side of the altar. And that's when we took off the other way and got caught by the security guard."

Sister Bernadette holds up the stop sign. "I've heard enough. Strange men wandering in the church; girls— girls who should have been *home*—hiding under tables. I understand that Father Julian vouched for you, and that's why Father Danahey let you go."

"Sister, we didn't have anything to do with those missing candlesticks," Margaret says. "I swear. We would never steal anything, especially from a church."

"I think I missed something," says a bewildered Mr. Eliot.

"A pair of valuable candlesticks disappeared from the altar yesterday," explains Sister Bernadette.

Mr. Eliot raises one eyebrow, first at me, then at Margaret.

"C'mon, Mr. Eliot. You know we'd never do anything like that," I say.

Mr. Eliot sighs. Deeply. "Sister, I do know these two pretty well, and I really don't think they could have had anything to do with something like that. Of course, that doesn't excuse their sneaking around the church after closing, but—"

"All right, all right. But I can't let that go completely unpunished. I take it that they are both taking part in your Dickens event, Mr. Eliot?"

"Unfortunately," he answers.

"Well, I'll suspend their punishment until after that, but starting Monday you each have one week's detention. The last thing I need around here is Father Danahey breathing down my neck because my girls are running wild in the church. In the meantime, STAY OUT of the church. Thank you, Mr. Eliot. You may all leave." She just about shoves us out of her office.

"All right," says Mr. Eliot when we are out of hearing range of the principal's office. "What haven't you told me? And by the way, I seem to remember you promising me that you weren't going to go sneaking around the church."

"Actually," Margaret says, "we promised not to *break into* the church. We never said anything about sneaking around."

"Staying out of trouble was the main idea, Miss Semantics. So, talk to me. Did you find the ring?" He is excited!

Margaret smiles. "We're *really* close."

"And?"

"And you'll just have to wait and see. I don't want to jinx it any more than I already have."

"Just promise me, please, to not get yourselves arrested."

"We prom-ise, Mis-ter El-i-ot," we singsong, running up the stairs, where we spend the next hour and a half on our *Great Expectations* skit. I kind of hope it is going to take my mind off of, well, everything. I do momentarily forget about my bag, but it isn't easy being around Leigh Ann. I can admit it: I act like a complete rhymes-with-witch to her during our rehearsal. She is trying to get me to give Herbert a stronger British accent, and I'm just not feeling it. She pushes and pushes, and I finally snap.

"Jeez, Leigh Ann, what *difference* does it make? It's just a stupid skit for a stupid fake banquet. Get off my back and out of my face!"

I don't mean it, not all of it. God, she looks crushed.

"Maybe we should just quit the whole thing," she says.

Margaret gives me a what-is-the-*matter*-with-you look and then turns to reassure Leigh Ann. "We are *not* quitting. This is a *great* scene, thanks to you, and even if we don't win, we can still have fun. Isn't that important, too? Sophie just has a lot on . . . what's left of her mind. Let's move on to the next part, after Herbert leaves. Sophie's going to take a little walk and try to purge some of her stress—aren't you, Sophie? And while you're at it, call Rebecca and see if she's on her way."

I skulk off and call Rebecca. She had gone home right after school to drop her brother and sister at an aunt's so she could come back for the Malcolm meeting and, if all goes well, to stay at my apartment for the night.

"This had better be worth it," she says. "I'm going to be babysitting my aunt's kid for the next year for free."

"The biter?"

"Yep."

And I thought I had problems.

At four-fifteen, four glum-faced, red-blazered girls shuffle into Perkatory and take seats around an unsteady round table. Margaret pulls up an extra chair, and we wait silently for Malcolm.

The girl behind the counter, a redhead in a Hunter College sweatshirt, greets us. "Hi, guys. What's with all the long faces?"

Margaret tries to be cheerful in spite of all the opposition. "Long day, long faces."

"You wouldn't have a Sophie at this table, would you?" she asks.

I lift my head. "Yeah, I'm Sophie."

"Somebody was in looking for you about an hour ago. Really cute guy. Said his name was . . . Ralph, er, Raf? Does that sound right? Waited around for a while, then said he had to go."

"You sure he was tooking for me? Not *her*?" I point my poison-arrow finger at Leigh Ann.

"Why would he be looking for me?" Leigh Ann asks, a perplexed look on her face.

I glare at her. "You're going out with him, aren't you?"

"With Raf? What gave you that idea?"

"The phone call? Remember? I was there when he called. I saw his number on your phone when I handed it to you."

"Yeah, I remember—he did call me, but I'm not going out with him. He called me for his *friend* Sean. I met him at the dance last week, and I guess he's kinda shy, so he got Rafael to call and ask me out for him."

Waves of about eight different emotions swell up and crash on the beach of my feeble brain. Rebecca thwumps me with her sketchbook. Margaret shakes her head and waggles her eyebrows at me.

"What is going on?" Leigh Ann asks, looking at us one by one.

"Sophie was mad at you," Margaret starts, "because she likes Raf, and she thought you were going out with him. Which is crazy, because even if you were, I practically heard her give you permission."

"Wait a second. This was all about Raf?" Leigh Ann tries to piece it together in her mind. "You know, I thought you were being kind of mean to me. If you like him, why didn't you just say something?"

"Because I'm a moron. God, I am so embarrassed."

"You should be," Rebecca says. "Who else thinks Sophie should buy the first round?"

The girl behind the counter raises her hand along with Rebecca, Margaret, and Leigh Ann, and then says, "How 'bout four of my specialty—a mocha float. It's got coffee, chocolate, and ice cream. I'll give 'em to you for half price."

"Leigh Ann, I am so sorry. It's just that, well, you guys would make like the *perfect* couple."

"Except he likes *you*, and you like him, and I don't like him. Not like that."

"He doesn't like me."

"You'll never convince her, Leigh Ann," says Margaret.

"Am I interrupting something?" Malcolm suddenly materializes next to our table.

Margaret spins in her seat to face him.

Malcolm points to his shoes. "Soft soles. Better for sneaking about." That sly, sly smile. But no smirk in sight.

I take a whiff; he is using the same stuff on his hair, and I'm still not sure I want my fate in hands that smell like the locker room after gym class.

Margaret points him to the empty chair. "Thanks for coming. Especially on such short notice."

I check the door again. "Are you sure nobody followed you?"

This makes him chuckle, and for the first time, I see a twinkle in his eye—a twinkle that says: I'm not quite the bad guy you think I am.

Could I have been wrong? Again!

"My, my. Should I have been expecting someone to follow me? I had no idea I had wandered into such a shady underworld."

"She's just a little nervous," Margaret says. "There's really just one person in particular that we would rather not know about this meeting. Sophie had kind of a bad experience this morning with someone from last night."

"Let me guess: Gordon Winterbottom."

"How did you know?" Maybe he *can* help me.

Malcolm chuckles again. "Well, of all the people present last night, he's the one I wouldn't want following *me*. I don't blame you for being concerned about Mr. Winterbottom. As a matter of fact, *I'm* very concerned about him myself, for reasons I needn't go into right now. But tell me—what kind of bad experience are we talking about?"

Margaret takes a deep breath. "Okay, we're going to

tell you something, because we need your help, but I don't know if we have anything to offer you in return— so we're just going to have to take a chance that you'll do the right thing."

Malcolm calmly folds his hands on the table in front of us. "Before you start, are you sure it is the *right* thing that you want me to do? Or is it merely the thing you *want* me to do? Are you sure they are one and the same?"

Oy. If he calls us young grasshoppers, I'm leaving.

Zen Master Margaret states her case: "Let me put it this way. To the best of my *knowledge*, it is the right thing. However, if my understanding of the facts is flawed, it is entirely possible that what truly is right and what we want, based on the information we now have, are *not* the same."

"Fair enough. Girls, I'm going to go out on a limb here and guess that this has something to do with the item we discussed last Saturday at the Met. An object aptly described by your young male friend as 'the stuff that dreams are made of.' Am I right?" We nod, and he continues. "And I'm going to climb a bit further out on that same limb by suggesting that our mutual friend Mr. Winterbottom has developed a keen interest in said item."

"Did he say something to you about it?"

"Oh, no. Gordon's much too clever for that. You see, there's something about him that you don't know. From the moment I met you girls in Elizabeth's foyer and got wind of what you were up to, I feared that this very situation would result."

"But why?"

"Because every time you visited Elizabeth, he knew *exactly* what was said."

"How? Does he have the place bugged or something?"

"Nothing that sophisticated. What he has is a spy. Someone 'on the inside,' as you spy types say. Elizabeth's housekeeper, Winifred—"

"I knew it!" I shout.

"She is Gordon's wife."

"His *wife*?" Margaret says. "We thought she was working with *you*. Isn't she a *lot* younger than he is?"

"Gordon is younger than he looks."

Margaret looks concerned. "So he isn't bluffing. He really does know."

"What, exactly, does he know?"

"That we found the ring."

Malcolm straightens up, eyes wide. "You *found* it? How? Where? Where is it? Can I see it?"

Margaret tells him the greatly abridged version and then has me give him the details of my private meeting with Winterrump.

"We need access to the church when we can be absolutely certain that no one *will* be around," Margaret says. "That's where *you* come in."

"I see. Ah, and am I correct in deducing that the 'right thing' that you want me to do is to let you recover the ring and return it to my ex-wife."

. "Something like that."

Malcolm rubs his chin, moving his gaze around the table at the four of us. "What if I told you that I have an even better, more equitable solution? Why not give the ring directly to Caroline? After all, from what you have told me, it *was* intended as her birthday present. I can tell you that she will be eternally grateful to have this last gift from her grandfather."

"I don't know," said Margaret. "We kind of promised Elizabeth. I'm not sure we can—"

"Leave that part to me. In fact, this meeting helps me better understand the conversation I had with Elizabeth just this morning. It seems that, after fifteen years, she has a sudden urge to speak to our daughter again. Actually, we had quite a lovely talk, the most civil discussion we've had in many years. In addition to finding the ring, you girls may be responsible for getting a family back on speaking terms."

Margaret and I share a quick look at each other, fighting back smiles. Malcolm has played the "family card" for us. "If it is okay with Ms. Harriman, it is okay with us."

Our business complete, Becca and Leigh Ann go up to the counter to order a second mocha float, and Margaret wanders off to the bathroom, leaving me alone with Malcolm.

He leans over, talking softly. "I have an idea, Miss St. Pierre. A way to bring this episode to a close with a little panache. I have in mind a particularly *inspired* piece of theater—but I need you to play the lead. Are your acting skills up to snuff?"

I lean in, nodding enthusiastically, and smile as he reveals the details of his plan, which we agree to keep between the two of us.

When the others return to the table, Malcolm gives me a quick wink and then tells us all to go home, relax for a couple of hours, and wait for his e-mail. We shake hands with our surprising new co-conspirator, who then does something *really* nice—he picks up the check!

Chapter 32

In which I learn that gold houses, superpowers, and Maseratis are nothing compared to good friends

When we leave Perkatory a little after five, we are in *much* better spirits, but most importantly, we are a team again, even though Rebecca refuses to wear her blazer outside the walls of the school. As *un artiste,* she feels compelled to demonstrate her individuality by wearing a faded, stained denim jacket.

I am surprised and somewhat concerned that both of my parents are home. Dad is usually only home on Sunday and Monday nights, and a Thursday is practically unheard of.

"Dad? What are you doing home?" As soon as I say it, I realize how it must sound.

"What kind of greeting is that for someone who has kindly brought you and your friends these delectable pastries? Maybe your mother and I will just eat them all instead."

"Éclairs? Really? *Papa, tu es le meilleur.*"

"How was your day?" Mom asks.

"Well, it started off a little rough, but it just keeps getting better and better. Mom, I have the best friends *ever*. And, um, I think I forgot to tell you, but these guys are gonna stay here tonight. Remember, the banquet thing is tomorrow, and we're still working on our skit. You're coming, right?"

"Absolutely. And your dad is going to try to make it, if he's not too busy at the restaurant."

I have no idea how we are going to sneak out past both of them tonight—especially since Dad is likely to be up reading or watching TV in the living room until all hours. Turns out, though, that it is movie night at the St. Pierre house. My parents go out to the movies maybe once or twice a year—and this is one of those nights. It is Dad's turn to pick the movie, and because he's French, it is certain to be something dark, depressing, and foreign—which means they are heading downtown, where all the "artsy" theaters are, which in turn means that we have a window of at least three hours to do everything we need to do. Plenty of time—as long as Malcolm comes through at a reasonable hour.

As soon as we pile into my bedroom, Margaret goes online to check her e-mail, and sure enough, there it is:

Dear Girls-in-Red-Blazers,
Liftoff! Red door, 8:45 PM—sharp!

Await further instructions inside.

MC

Not a wasted syllable.

Margaret turns to me, smiling. "We're going to do it, Soph."

"I want to believe, Margaret."

" 'Great deeds are usually wrought at great risks.' Herodotus." She can't resist.

If I were really clever, or read the kind of books Margaret reads, I would have a snappy comeback for that line. Why didn't Elmer Fudd or Daffy Duck ever say anything profound?

Mom sticks her head in my room. "Is everything all right in here? If you girls are hungry, Sophie's dad made his famous macaroni and cheese; it's in the oven, and the éclairs are in the fridge. Our show doesn't start until nine-fifteen, so we won't be back till after midnight. Don't stay up too late, okay? You all have a big day tomorrow. Margaret, you're sensible; make sure Sophie gets some sleep, okay? We don't want her dozing onstage."

"No problem, Kate."

I kiss Mom on the cheek. "Bye, *Kate*. Have fun at the depressing movie."

"You know, Sophie, not all French films are depressing," she says, loud enough for Dad to hear. Then she whispers, "But this one sounds like a real doozy. I have extra tissues, just in case."

The second they are out the door, we ransack the kitchen, polishing off a huge dish of macaroni and cheese, which Leigh Ann declares is the best thing she has ever eaten. "Holy cannoli, Sophie. Can I just move in with you? Your parents can adopt me and in exchange I'll clean the kitchen like nobody's business. We can be sisters. I can't believe your dad made that. My dad can't even make toast."

It is the first time I have heard Leigh Ann mention her dad. "Are your parents, um, together?"

"No, they got divorced when I was in third grade, but it's okay, because I still see him a lot. He lives a few blocks away from us in Astoria."

"Hey, I have a question for all of you," Margaret announces as we spread out in my room. "You know the legend of the ring, right? How if you wear the ring, St. Veronica appears in your dreams and answers your prayers. Think about this—we are going to *have* that ring in a couple of hours. So, my question is: what would *you* ask for? And it has to be something *possible,* something *good.* No superpowers or a house made out of gold or things like that."

"What if I use the superpowers to fight crime?" Rebecca asks. "That would be good, wouldn't it? And if the people I save want to thank me with a house of gold . . ."

"I'd like for my parents to get back together," says Leigh Ann. "I know it's kind of a cliché, but with my parents, at least it *seems* possible. When they were together, everything was so much . . . easier. Not just for me, but for my mom, too. And my dad seemed happier then, too. Is that a stupid thing to hope for?"

I reach over and pat her on the shoulder. "I think it's totally sweet. I can't even imagine what it would be like if my parents got divorced. Becca, what about you? Seriously."

"Well, I was *going* to say I wanna be able to fly, but I guess that's no good, and the whole 'world peace' thing has been done to death, so I guess I'll go with something simple. I want to see my dad again, even if it's just in my dreams. You know, maybe just to live one day over again with him. I was only seven when he died, so I hardly remember him, and I never dream about him anymore. It's funny, I remember how he smelled—like the ink from his print shop—more than how he looked. That's what I'd like. That, and a house made of gold. And a Maserati. They're cool. And if I had either one of those, I wouldn't mind not being able to fly."

"That's like Emily," Margaret says. "You know, from *Our Town*. The first part, not the gold house and the Maserati. Only in her case, it's after she dies that she gets to relive one day of her life."

Rebecca looks a little confused. "Isn't it kinda too late by then?"

"I think that was the point," I say.

Leigh Ann nudges me. "Okay, Sophie. Your turn."

"Oh, I think we all know what *she* wants," Rebecca teases.

"Shut up, Rebecca. I'm still thinking, but *not* about what you think. Margaret, you go ahead of me."

"Well, if I had to decide right this second, I would copy Rebecca. I want to live my eighth birthday over again. That was the last time I saw my grandfather. We moved to America a couple of months later, and he died about a year after that. I had so much fun that day. He played the piano and we all sang and danced, and the food—oh my gosh. It was the *perfect* day."

Sometimes it's kind of intimidating having friends like mine. "Wow. Yours are all so . . . nice. I don't know."

"Don't try to weasel out of this, Zoltan," Rebecca says.

"There must be something you want," Leigh Ann adds.

I think about the dream I had about Raf driving me home in his convertible, but then I look around the room at my three best friends. And I know exactly what I want more than anything else in the world.

"I want us to stay friends forever. I don't want anything to come between us. Not boys or other friends. Not moving away because of our parents' jobs. Not college or careers."

I am a sap. And a dork. I'm a sork.

Group hug.

Before we know it, it is eight o'clock. Time to rock.

Field Marshall Margaret assumes command of her troops. "Sophie, do you have a flashlight? The church is going to be really dark."

I rummage through a kitchen drawer until I find a cheap flashlight. I hold it up triumphantly, clicking it on and off.

"Good. Now, is everyone wearing sneakers?"

"We could all wear black slacks and turtlenecks, and darken our faces. Or is that overkill?" Rebecca asks.

"Our regular clothes are fine," Margaret says. "And I think I have all the tools we'll need in my bag."

"I'm a little confused," says Leigh Ann. "If this Malcolm guy is going to help us, then why do we have to sneak around? Why can't we just get the ring and leave?"

Rebecca agrees. "Yeah, that's a good point. Why do we even need to worry about Winterbooty? I mean, what can he do if our new best buddy Malcolm is there with us?"

I smile to myself. *I* know exactly why, but I'm not letting on—at least not yet. "I'm sure he has his reasons. He's probably afraid ol' Winterbutt will call the cops or something. Let's just get moving."

We ring the doorbell at precisely eight-forty-five, and Ms. Harriman answers the door herself, wearing an orangey floral-print skirt that clashes *hard* with her red blazer and talking a mile a minute.

"Hello, girls! My, isn't this exciting? I feel like I'm in the middle of a spy novel. I wore my red blazer for good luck. Malcolm explained what is going to happen. I don't know *what* I'll do about Winnie when this is all over. To tell you the truth, I was never crazy about the way she cleaned anyway. She never once moved the furniture to vacuum underneath. Not once! Come in, have a seat, and I'll get us all some tea."

Margaret follows her to the kitchen. "Malcolm, er, Dr. Chance said that we should wait here for further instructions. Is he coming?"

"Oh, I'm sure—"

She is interrupted by a knock at the upstairs door.

"Oh, that must be him now! Sophie, would you mind answering the door?"

"Sure." I bound up the steps. A moment of panic follows; what if it is Winterbottom?

I open the door, holding my breath, eyes barely open. It is Father Julian, grinning and looking weirdly young in jeans and a Fordham sweatshirt.

"We meet again, Miss St. Pierre."

"Father Julian. I wasn't expecting—well, I don't know what I was expecting, but I don't think you were even on the list. Come on in; everyone else is downstairs."

He takes a seat in the living room. "First, let me just say: wow! This really has been *some* adventure for you girls. Dr. Chance brought me up to speed this afternoon and asked me to give you a hand. He'll be at the Parish Council meeting, which starts in a few minutes, which will also tie up Mr. Winterbottom for at least an hour. Dr. Chance intends to involve him in a lengthy discussion about the importance of maintaining the church's treasures. My instructions are to take you girls downstairs and into the church at exactly nine o'clock. Once we get there, you will have to work fast; he can't guarantee how long he can keep Mr. Winterbottom occupied. Sophie, I heard about the conversation you had with Mr. Winterbottom this morning, and I can't tell you how sorry I am that you had to go through that. Rest assured, we will deal with him."

Margaret is helping Ms. Harriman pour the tea. "Elizabeth, when you first found that card in that book of poems, did you ever imagine all these things happening?"

"Well, no, but I do love surprises! This little adventure has transported me back in time to my own childhood and my travels with Father. And best of all, I've gotten to know you girls."

"I just can't wait to touch the ring," I say. "I mean, somebody made it almost two *thousand* years ago. Think how different their lives were from ours."

Ms. Harriman shakes her head. "Maybe not as different as you think. Families, love, life, quarrels, death. Those things haven't changed much, I think."

The grandfather clock in her hallway begins to chime; it is nine o'clock.

Father Julian stands and looks around. "Are you all ready?"

We all look at each other and nod vigorously. Ms. Harriman wishes us luck, and Father Julian leads us up the stairs and into the passageway.

Chapter 33

Sometimes a little spit is all you need

We creep down the back staircase, fingers and toes crossed against the chance that we will run into any kind of obstacle. Margaret and Father Julian lead the way, and we stop when we get to our old friend, the door with the stained glass chalice. Margaret takes a deep breath, turns the knob, and pushes it open. This is it, the big moment. The church is *really* dark. There are a few "night lights" plugged into sockets, but the dim light they give off is absorbed by the cold stone walls. Statues of Jesus and Mary and the saints seem to come to life as we creep past them in the darkness, their limbs reaching out to us as our shadows flicker over them.

Gradually our eyes adjust to the darkness, and I make out the figure of Father Julian motioning for us to come closer. My heart is thumpa-ka-thumping like mad.

Margaret waves us on. "Okay, let's do it."

All of us, including Father Julian, are wearing sneakers, so we silently make our way from the door to the altar. All that effort is wasted, however, when I drop the flashlight—which instantly shatters into a million pieces, with the batteries spinning and skidding wildly across the polished marble floor. You just cannot believe how long the sound waves bounce around those stone walls. Around and around they go, while all I can do is cringe. Finally, *finally,* it stops.

"Please tell me that wasn't the only flashlight," whispers Father Julian as we all crouch low, half waiting for who-knows-what.

Margaret, ever the good Girl Scout, puts her hand on my back. "It's okay, Soph. I've got a little light here on my key chain. I bought it right after that first day with Raf."

Have I mentioned how lucky I am friend-wise?

Father Julian sizes up the altar table. "All right. Which leg is it?"

"This one right here," Margaret says. "It's centered right over the intersection of the four tiles. We only have to move it over about a foot—just enough so we can get to all the tiles. What do you think? Can we do it?"

Rebecca pushes against it, groaning, but nothing happens. She shakes her head. "Man, I've never seen a table like this. No way."

"We have to lift and push at the same time." I hope my positive attitude will make up for that unfortunate flashlight incident.

Father Julian agrees. "I think Sophie's right. Let's give it a try."

The five of us line up on one side of the table.

"One, two, three, PUSH!" Margaret orders. We might as well be pushing against the outside wall of the church.

Rebecca looks at the bottom of her shoes. "I'm slipping on this stuff. They must have just waxed it or something."

I slide my feet around on the smooth marble. "Me too. We need some spit."

"Excuse me?" Even in the darkness I can see the horrified look on Father Julian's face.

"Spit. You spit on the bottom of your shoes, or you spit on the floor and then rub your shoes in it. Makes them sticky. Basketball players do it all the time."

"Can we please step off the altar to do this?"

"What? Ohhhhhh. Yeah. I'm sorry, I just wasn't—"

"It's all right. Let's all just give it a try."

What a difference a little traction makes. We're not fast, and it doesn't go far, but by grunting and groaning, and pushing and pulling, we move that behemoth just enough to clear the four tiles. As we kneel down around the tile, Father Julian shushes us for a second, looking around the church interior. He then crosses himself. After a quick look at each other, we all do it, too. (Hey, it can't hurt.)

Margaret feels around the edge of the first of the

polished stone squares, looking for a place to grip. "Boy, it's in here pretty tight. There's definitely no cement in between it and the other tiles, though." She then unzips her backpack and holds up a thin piece of metal, bent at one end.

"What's that?"

"I don't know what it's called; it's for opening paint cans or something. Figured it might come in handy."

"What else do you have in that bag of yours?" marvels Father Julian.

Rebecca snorts. "A forklift. A miniature nuclear reactor. One of those inflatable swimming pools. Grappling hook. Lipstick ray gun."

Margaret slides the thinnest end of the tool into the crevice that appears to be the widest. Then, gently, gently, gently, she starts prying, moving the tool from side to side, working it under the edge. I pray (along with Father Julian, I'm sure) that the tile doesn't crack. Does she have a spare slab of matching marble in that magic bag of hers?

"Here we go," she says as the edge of the tile starts to rise. "Just . . . a . . . little . . . bit . . . further . . . and . . . Got it!" Her eyes sparkle with excitement.

"Careful," Father Julian cautions.

Margaret reaches her hands under the tile and then she and Father Julian lift it clear of its home.

We are all on our knees, practically bumping heads in what looks like some bizarre religious ritual. Rebecca points the light into the hole where the tile had spent the last twenty years undisturbed. Margaret's hands glide around the space, but there is no sign of anything unusual.

She doesn't seem at all worried. "It's okay. That's just one tile. Three more to check. It could be under any of them."

"Well, at least the others ought to be easy to get out," Rebecca observes. "The first one was the tough one."

Suddenly a light comes on in the dressing room just off the altar, and we freeze. Voices—men's voices—and they are *close*.

"Quick, under the table," says Father Julian, and for the second time in just over twenty-four hours, I am hiding under the altar table in St. Veronica's Church. With five of us, it is incredibly crowded. Leigh Ann is practically on top of me, and I can feel her breath on the back of my neck as I listen to footsteps approaching.

"You see, Gordon, there's no one here." It is the unmistakable voice of Malcolm Chance. "It's as quiet as a church." He is standing next to the table; one of his familiar shoes is covering the corner of the gap where the missing tile had been just moments before.

"I tell you, I heard something," Winterbottom replies.

"Everything's locked up as tight as a drum. I checked the doors myself. You probably just heard something from outside on the street. Come on, let's go back inside. I have one more set of figures to run past you; I think it's time to renovate the convent, and we need to come up with some money."

Winterbutthead grunts. I can tell he isn't completely satisfied with Malcolm's explanation, but he follows him out of the church anyway. We wait until the light is switched off and the door pulled shut behind them before we dare to move.

"My, that was close." Father Julian breathes deeply.

I agree wholeheartedly. "Yeah. Let's get this done and get out of here."

Margaret slides her paint can tool under the second tile, which lifts right out. In the center of that square is another square, about two inches on each side, which has been neatly dug down into the floor beneath the tiles. The hole is just deep enough, in fact, to hold a small black jewel box—the kind that rings come in.

"Holy crap," I say. "Sorry, Father."

"No, I agree. Holy crap, indeed."

"Open it, open it," hisses Rebecca.

"Father Julian, you do the honors," Margaret says.

"No, no, no. You girls did all the work. You deserve it."

"Go for it, Margaret," I whisper.

She pries the box out of the hole and holds it under the light for us all to see. Grasping it with both hands, she carefully lifts the lid.

Pressed into the purple velvet lining is a ring

exactly like the one we saw in the Metropolitan Museum. It is absolutely perfect, and the gold and rubies glimmer and sparkle in the light from Margaret's tiny flashlight.

Leigh Ann's mouth is open in awe. "It's amazing."

"The stuff dreams are made of," I say. "What do you think, Margaret?"

"I think it's the most beautiful thing I've ever seen."

Father Julian breaks the spell. "Okay, we need to get out of here. Let's get the tiles back in place and hope that we have the strength to move this table one more time."

Margaret picks up the tile and is about to set it in place when I stop her. "Wait. There's something I have to do." I reach into the pocket of my jeans and take out a folded piece of construction paper.

"What's that?"

"Just a friendly little note."

"For whom?" Margaret quizzes.

"Why, Mr. Winterjerk, of course. Margaret, you didn't think we were done with him yet, did you?"

"Well, I just kind of figured—"

"That once we had the ring, we were done? We have a golden—pun *totally* intended—opportunity to really mess with ol' Winterslime. This is a little something Malcolm and I cooked up. Let me have the box the ring is in."

"Why?"

"Don't argue. Give it to me. Just the box. Trust me. I know what I'm doing."

Margaret carefully removes the two-thousand-year-old ring from its slot in the velvet lining and hands the empty box to me. I turn so no one can see what I am doing. Then I snap the lid shut and hand it back to Margaret with a satisfied smile. "All done."

She sets the box in its indentation in the floor and ever so gently replaces the two tiles. When she finishes, she looks up at me with a sly grin.

The table seems lighter the second time we have to move it. Maybe it is all that adrenaline rushing through us? But rather than returning it to the exact spot it had been in, I convince everyone to place it so that it is possible to access the ring's hiding place. Then we clean up all the broken flashlight parts and take one last look. It is absolutely impossible to tell that anything has been tampered with.

As we slip through the door with the chalice (the "Holy Grail Door," as Rebecca refers to it), we thank Father Julian one last time and climb the stairs to the entrance to Ms. Harriman's.

"Mission accomplished!" I shout as she opens the door.

Her face beams, and she hugs us all, thanking us over and over again. We show her the ring, and she starts to cry—just a few tears, but enough to make us feel bad for her and try to comfort her.

"Oh, no, no, girls, I'm not crying because I'm sad. This little ring represents so much. My father, my daughter. And my granddaughter. Even Malcolm, that old coot. But look who's talking. What an old fool I've been. What if I've waited too long—"

The doorbell rings and she collects herself, swiping the tears away and pausing in front of a mirror to check her hair and makeup. It is Malcolm, who gives her a quick peck on the cheek and then gestures to us, palms up and eyebrows raised. He has to know from our glowing faces that we have been successful, but he still asks: "Well?"

Margaret is standing there with her chin held high. "Right where I said it would be."

"Excellent. May I see it?"

"You may indeed. We couldn't have done this without you."

"When that light came on in the church, I thought we were cooked," I say.

Malcolm chuckles. "You and me both. What *was* that awful racket? It sounded like someone kicked over a bucket of marbles."

"Sophie dropped her flashlight."

"She's smooth," Rebecca says.

"No harm done. Just a few anxious moments." He holds the ring up to the light, admiring it. "It's even more beautiful than I remembered."

He hands the ring back to Margaret. "You found it; you get to take care of it for one more day."

"Are you sure?" She holds it out, Frodo-like, in the palm of her hand.

"I am. Now, I understand that you girls are all taking part in some kind of theatrical event at the school tomorrow night—am I right? Good. Elizabeth and I will both be present." He turns to Ms. Harriman and smiles. "As will two very special guests."

Her eyes turn watery again. "Thank you, Malcolm."

"When the performance is over, please come and see us. That will, perhaps, be an appropriate time for you to give the ring directly to its *rightful* owner."

"You mean—"

"Tomorrow. But right now, unless I'm mistaken, you young people should all be home in bed. It *is* a school night, and, well, you're not really delinquents, true?"

"Oh, no—we're *very* good girls," Rebecca says.

As we edge toward the door, I nudge Malcolm on the arm. "Are we still on for tomorrow?"

"Ah, the coup de grâce. Absolutely! Go ahead and meet Mr. Winterbottom at seven o'clock as directed. I take it that, uh, *everything* went according to plan in the church tonight?"

"Perfectly. Well, except for that exploding flashlight thing."

Margaret turns around to face me. "What are you two talking about? Sophie St. Pierre. After all we've been through! Are you keeping something from me?"

"Only a very little thing. You'll see soon enough."

"And when did you arrange all this?"

"At Perkatory, when Leigh Ann and Becca were up at the counter and you went to the bathroom."

"Serves me right. The most interesting stuff *always* happens when you're in the bathroom."

Chapter 34

In which I give the performance of a lifetime. Cue the "APPLAUSE" sign!

We leave Ms. Harriman's in a hurry and get back to my apartment at about ten-fifteen. I check with Kevin, our doorman, to make sure my parents haven't returned yet and beg him not to mention my own late-ish arrival. They get home just *minutes* after us; they had a change of heart about the movie and went out for a little late dinner instead. If we had spent five more minutes at Ms. Harriman's or had stopped for a slice of pizza (like the perpetually hungry Rebecca had suggested!), we would have been busted.

It is going to be a *long* time before anybody goes to sleep, even though we are all exhausted. We pass the ring back and forth, admiring it on our fingers while re-hashing the whole adventure. Sometime between midnight and one, we start to slow down, but before we crash, we have a very important decision to make. Which one of us should wear the ring to sleep?

Rebecca shuffles a deck of cards several times and then fans them out on the floor. Leigh Ann draws the five of hearts, Rebecca the jack of spades, and Margaret the two of diamonds. I reach for a card and flip it over. The king of diamonds. Cha-ching.

"Everybody's okay with this?" I ask.

"It's perfect," Margaret says. "If the legend of the ring is true, we'll all be friends forever."

At three-forty-four a.m., I sit up suddenly in bed. I could have sworn someone shook me awake, but Margaret, next to me on the bed, is sleeping soundly, and so are Leigh Ann and Rebecca, on the air bed in the middle of the floor. I take the ring off my finger, slip it onto Margaret's left pinkie, roll over, and go back to sleep.

The screech of the alarm clock wakes us. Margaret and I sit up partway and throw our pillows at Rebecca, who has buried her head beneath hers.

A few seconds later, Leigh Ann sits up. She even looks good in the morning, damn it. "Um, Sophie?"

"Yeah?"

She holds up her left hand with a puzzled look. The ring is on her second finger. "Did you—"

"It wasn't me." I scratch my head, trying to recall the events of the night. "It was the strangest thing. I re-member waking up at three-forty-four. I looked right at the clock, and then I took the ring off and put it on Margaret's finger. But what's really weird is that I don't remember thinking 'I should give this to Margaret' or anything like that. I just did it. It was automatic, like I was *programmed* to do it or something."

"Okay, I just got goose bumps," Margaret says. "Because the exact same thing happened to me! I woke up at four-thirty-seven and put it on Rebecca's finger. And now that I think about it, I don't even remember wondering how it got on *my* finger. I just did it. And then I had this dream . . ."

Rebecca slowly pulls the pillow from her face, squinting at the light. "It happened to me at five-nineteen. I thought you guys were goofing around, because it felt like someone was shaking me. And I gave it to Leigh Ann."

Leigh Ann stares at the ring. "That is *freaky*. When the alarm went off I was having a dream. I can only remember bits and pieces, but it felt so *real*. And I have this strange feeling that it isn't over. It's like I *know* I'll have the dream again."

We all look at each other and nod. We know *exactly* what she is talking about.

Definition of chaos: four girls trying to get ready for school at the same time in an apartment with only one bathroom. Luckily, Dad slept in; he would have gone crazy with all the confusion and running around. Mom makes us breakfast and then, for her own safety, stays out of our way.

At six-thirty, I announce, "We need to be moving along, guys. Mom, thanks for breakfast. I'll see you at the banquet tonight. Dad *is* going to be there, isn't he?"

"He's going to meet me at seven-thirty. I've told him that your skit is first, so if he's late, he'll miss you, but he insists he'll be on time. Tell me again why you have to be at school at seven o'clock this morning?"

"We just have another, um, *project* that we need to finish up. It's due today, and we have a few little details to work on."

"Well, all right, but be careful; it's still dark out there."

"We're walking together, Mom. We'll be fine. See you tonight." I kiss her on the way out the door, and we are off.

The sky over the East River is glowing red and orange, and the air is crisp and cool. We have plenty of time to get to the church for my appointment with Winterbottom, so we decide to walk the whole way. At the door to Perkatory, I send Margaret, Leigh Ann, and Rebecca inside with my assurance that I will be back before they have finished their coffees.

Margaret's arms are crossed. "Are you *sure* you don't want us to come with you?"

I shake my head. "Don't worry. I'll be fine. He's

going to be ticked off, sure, but what's he going to do? The only thing I need is that little tool you used last night to lift the tile."

Margaret finds it in her bag and hands it to me. "Good luck. And remember, go slowly—don't break the tiles."

"Got it. Nice and easy."

"And, Soph? Don't drop it."

Gordon Winterbottom is waiting for me in the foyer of the church, pacing with a pained look on his icky face. I glance around the barely lit church interior. No one else around. No security guard, no construction workers, no little old ladies waiting for Mass. Just me and Gross Greedy.

"Ready?" Apparently we aren't bothering with any pleasantries.

Time for my close-up. Quiet on the set, please.

"Y-yeah, I'm ready. Look, m-mister, please, let's get this over with so I can get my bag and get out of here. I don't want to get into any trouble. I don't even care about the stupid ring anymore."

"But you *do* know exactly where it is, right?"

"I—I know where it's *supposed* to be, according to my friend's calculations. But maybe she's not as smart as she thinks. And I mean, it *has* been twenty years. A lot of things can happen in that amount of time." We walk down the center aisle of the church; out of the corner of my eye I spy a piece of the flashlight I had dropped, which makes me chuckle to myself. I am also pretty sure I see the shadow of someone standing behind the familiar door with the stained glass chalice, which appears to be propped open. Friend or foe? I take out a piece of notebook paper with some scribbled notes, which I pretend to study with tremendous earnestness and then make a big show of counting out the tiles and finally arriving at *the* tile. "Okay, if the calculations are correct, it should be under this tile. Do you want me to lift it? I brought a little tool. Or do you want to do it?"

Winterbottom makes a series of faces and then grunts. "You do it. Go ahead. Come on, quickly."

I stick the edge of the tool into the crevice between the tiles, just as Margaret had done, gently wiggling it back and forth until it is far enough in to start lifting. As I inch my fingernails under it, he gets down on his hands and knees, pushing me aside roughly so he can finish the job himself. I stand up and move a few feet away so I can see the look on his face when he opens that box.

His eyes flash with anticipation as he reaches into the opening and lifts out the jewel box that holds his treasure. Still kneeling, he snaps the lid open. I watch his jaw drop, just barely at first, and then, as the terrible realization of the situation hits him, more and more. Trembling and twitching, he holds up *not* the hoped-for Ring of Rocamadour but my four-buck, 1970s-vintage mood ring. The stone is a deathly gray in his hand. He glares at it for a second before dashing it to the floor. Then, my favorite part: he slowly unfolds my note—written across four paper dolls, joined at the hands, and each sporting a crimson St. Veronica's blazer. His face turns a shade of red I've never seen before (although tuna sashimi comes close). He looks up at me, and I am a *teensy* bit afraid. Is he going to kill me right here on the spot? Or just have a stroke?

But this is *my* moment. I give him my most diabolical smile and snap his picture with my phone, which, like me, is *fully* charged.

"Thank you," I say. "That look on your face is just *priceless*—really the stuff dreams are made of. Why, whatever is the matter, Mr. Winterbottom? You seem upset. Is it not what you expected to find?"

All he can manage is a grunt in my direction.

"I don't know about you, but I've found that lots of things in life are like that. You build things up in your mind, and then, when you finally find what it is you've been searching for, you're disappointed. I wonder why that is? It seems—"

"You think you're very clever, don't you?" He rises to his feet and tries to intimidate me.

Fat chance. "Actually, I *know* I'm pretty clever. Clever enough to outsmart you, you disgusting wannabe crook." I pick up my mood ring, which immediately begins to glow a very healthy and contented purple in my hand.

"This isn't over. Don't forget, I still have that precious bag of yours."

"Would this be the bag you're talking about?" says Malcolm, stepping up onto the altar, joined by Father Julian, who is holding up my book bag.

Mr. Winterbottom suddenly looks like a cornered rat. "I might have known you would be involved in this, Chance! You've always had it in for me. It was because of you that Everett Harriman didn't leave me anything in his will—after twenty years of loyal service. That ring belongs to me. I deserve it. I earned it!"

"Just like you deserve these?" Malcolm takes the candlesticks from my bag and places them on the altar table. "How many other church treasures have you stolen over the years, Gordon? All those missing items that we just chalked up to random thefts—how many of those were your handiwork?"

"How dare you. I have devoted my life to St. Veronica's. Do you honestly believe that Father Danahey is going to take your word over mine after all I've done?"

"*That* will be up to Father Danahey. But with Miss St. Pierre and Father Julian—"

"This, this juvenile delinquent!" Winterbottom scoffs. "You think Father Danahey is going to believe *anything* she says, after she was caught red-handed in the church, after closing time—with *those* in her bag? And we all know it's not even the first time."

"Even a third-class detective could tell you that the problem with that story is lack of motive. *Why* would she steal two very ordinary-looking candlesticks when they were *this* close to finding the ring? Look at them. She would have had no way of knowing they had any value; they look like they might have come from a ninety-nine-cent store. It just doesn't cut it."

Winterbottom's only response is to scowl at Malcolm, Father Julian, and me. He spins on his heel and stalks off toward the main entrance, shouting over his shoulder, "This isn't over!"

Of course, his exit would have been a little more dramatic if he didn't stop at the top of the steps to light a cigarette. While he's standing there, Winnie bolts out of the chalice door and bustles down the aisle after him, her shoes squeaking on the polished floor. When she catches up with him, she pounds her fists against his chest like a child having a tantrum. A pretty pathetic spectacle. I *almost* feel sorry for him.

Father Julian watches the two of them leave, shaking his head sadly. He asks how I am.

"Oh, I'm fine now. I was a little freaked out right before you two came in. He looked kind of scary."

He reaches down and picks up the jewelry box and the paper doll note and hands them to me. "Keepsakes of your little adventure."

"What does your note say, anyway?" asks Malcolm.

I show it to him.

DEAR MR. WINTERBOTTOM:

YOU HAVE JUST BEEN OUTSMARTED, OUTPLAYED, AND CAUGHT RED-HANDED BY

THE RED BLAZER GIRLS

"Beautiful. The Red Blazer Girls, eh? I like that."

Father Julian nods his approval. "Me too. It has a nice 'ring' to it, if you'll excuse the pun."

I will. Just this once.

When my book bag and I oh-so-casually stroll into Perkatory a few minutes later, my three best friends greet me like a conquering hero and demand the details.

"It was Malcolm's idea, really. He's been convinced for a long time that Winterbottom was stealing stuff from the church, but he couldn't prove it. This was our chance to really stick it to him. The mood ring was his idea, but *this* was mine." I stretched out the paper doll note on the table.

"That is so perfect," says Leigh Ann.

Margaret hugs me. "It's *so* perfect that I'm jealous I didn't think of it."

"Boy, he must be steamed," Rebecca says. "Getting his butt kicked by a bunch of kids."

"Yeah, I would give anything to have seen the look

on his face when he read this," Margaret says. "I *should* be mad at you for not letting us go with you. You could at least have taken a picture."

I slap my palm to my forehead. "Oh, man! I shoulda taken his picture! Can you *imagine* how awesome that woulda been? Like right at the moment he's reading the note?"

Everyone agrees: it's a shame. A pity, really. Coulda, woulda, shoulda.

I hold up my phone with a waggle of my eyebrows. Cut!

Chapter 35

Not really long enough to be a chapter, but after everything that happened in the last couple, I need a little break

I really hope my teachers don't say anything truly life-changing, because my classes are flying past like the blur of taxis speeding through a yellow light. I am running on adrenaline, caffeine, and about four hours less sleep than normal. I am *so* looking forward to a weekend-long crash. Only one obstacle remains—the Dickens banquet—and then I can sleep. Wonderful, glorious, sumptuous sleep.

We run through the skit one last time right after school, and Leigh Ann pronounces us officially ready. Rebecca and Margaret both promised to go home before the banquet, so Leigh Ann and I have some time to just hang out together, wandering through Bloomingdale's, sharing her iPod, and talking about you-know-who.

"Have you decided what to do about the boy?" she asks as we ride the escalator up to the shoe department.

"Because I feel a little responsible for, well, whatever is going on with you guys. I'm really sorry, Soph. I should have said something when he called me that day. If I had known—"

"No, I jumped to *all* kinds of conclusions."

"So now what?"

I make a face. "I dunno. I've been completely avoiding him for the past three days. He's been calling and texting, but I haven't returned any of them. He probably hates me by now."

"Somehow I doubt that. When he *stops* calling—that's when you should start to worry. Why don't you call him right now? What do you have to lose?"

"My mind? I mean, I'm kinda nervous about the skit, and I'm really tired. My brain's going to melt if I even try to think right now. If he shows up tonight—which I seriously doubt—I'll talk to him. For now, let's just have a look at some shoes. That doesn't require thinking."

That is, unless you're trying to calculate the cost of a cute pair of sandals that are 25 percent off their original price of $34.99, less another 15 percent, plus tax. I set them on the counter with $25 and cross my fingers.

So now what? I'm sure you're all wondering what will happen next. Will a bunch of seventh graders win the Dickens skit competition for the first time ever? Will Elizabeth and Malcolm—and their daughter, Caroline—

show up? Will they make up? And what about Raf? Will he surprise me by turning up after all? And what will I say to him? Should I save all this for a sequel? Put on something red and turn the page for just one more chapter. Pretty please.

Chapter 36

This is the one you've been waiting for

The curtain goes up, or over, or whatever it does, at seven-thirty sharp, and Mr. Eliot, wearing a rumpled, moth-eaten black coat with tails, a dusty top hat, and a fairly realistic beard, takes the stage at St. Veronica's twelfth annual Dickens of a Banquet. The guests are seated at round tables with white table-cloths and rented china and candlesticks while we wait in the stuffy, filthy space behind the stage. With the noise from the twenty-some girls with us, the whirring of the fans, and the constant clinking of silverware on plates, we miss most of Mr. Eliot's opening mono-logue, a mixture of Dickens's and his own "humor." C'est la vie.

An hour earlier, while Rebecca, Leigh Ann, and I waited for Margaret in the hallway outside the auditorium, we ran into Mr. Eliot and gave him the big news. He was really excited and wanted to see the ring, but it was with Margaret, who was uncharacteristically late. When she finally showed up, something was different about her. She hardly said anything, answering our questions with one- or two-word answers and managing only a forced, grim smile when Rebecca did her dead-on imitation of Mr. Eliot. She looked like she had been crying but insisted that she was fine. Margaret isn't like me. My emotions are right out there for everybody to see, but she holds most of hers in. When the time came to go backstage, she sat off by herself, staring at the toes of her shoes. Once every few minutes she took a small flowered card out of an envelope and read it in the dim light, slowly shaking her head.

Finally, I just can't take it anymore. "I'm gonna give it another try."

"You want us to come?" Rebecca asks.

"Give me a minute alone with her." I wander over and sit cross-legged on the floor in front of her.

After about a minute of silence, she says quietly, "I'm Pip."

"I know. And I'm Herbert. And Leigh Ann is Joe."

"I don't mean the skit."

"I don't understand."

"I *am* Pip." She finally makes eye contact with me. "I am not a good person."

"Margaret, what are you talking about? Is this some kind of Method acting thing? Are you just getting psyched up for our skit?"

"No, I really mean it. You should not be friends with me, Sophie. I am a poor excuse for a human being."

"That's ridiculous. You're an *amazing* human being and the best friend I've ever had. What are you talking about?"

"Read this." She hands me the envelope.

I remove the card and open it, but I can't read a word. "Is this Polish?"

She takes the card from my hand. "Oh, yeah. I forgot."

"What does it say?"

"It's an early Christmas present from my grand-mother. She's going back to Poland next week. Remember that violin camp in the Berkshires I told you about—the one I'm dying to go to next summer? Well, Mom told her about it, and she has been saving every penny for months. Yesterday she signed me up and paid for *everything*. And the worst part is, Mom told me that she even sold some of her jewelry, because she didn't have enough money. My parents offered to reimburse her for part of it, but she wanted it to be a special gift from her to her *special* granddaughter." Tears pour down Margaret's face, and she is shaking as she looks at the card again. She sobs as she reads, " 'Even when you're a famous violinist, you'll always be my little petunia.' That's what she called me when I was still in Poland. Her little petunia."

By now, Rebecca is next to me and Leigh Ann has her arms around the inconsolable Margaret.

"And look how I treated her. Just like Pip did with Joe."

"Margaret, this is crazy. You are not a bad person."

"And you know," Rebecca begins, "Pip turns out all right in the end. Hey, don't everybody look at me like that. I finished the book."

"That's right. I'm still not saying you're like him, but Pip knows he has made some mistakes, and he makes up for them by becoming the *real* Pip again, not the phony version he was in London. Look, you said your grandmother will be in town for another week, and then you guys will probably go to Poland at Easter, so you have lots of time. You can totally make it up to her."

Margaret's sad, wet eyes look up at me. "You really think so?"

"I do."

A snooty eighth-grade wannabe producer, carrying a clipboard and wearing one of those Britney-style headsets, interrupts us. "Aren't you guys the seventh graders? You're on in five. Oh, and good luck." She smirks.

She is exactly what we need to break our mood. We stand in a circle and put our hands in the center, with Margaret's left hand and the Ring of Rocamadour on top.

"For Margaret," I say.

"For us," Leigh Ann adds.

"For Frodo!" Rebecca cries, raising her fist.

We wait behind the curtain, listening to Mr. Eliot's introduction.

"This group of particularly brave girls are the only seventh graders in tonight's program. They have adapted the scene from *Great Expectations* in which Pip, who has moved to London to become a gentleman, is visited by Joe, his brother-in-law and closest friend from his humble childhood. In a rather short time, Pip has become a bit of a snob, and he is embarrassed by the country bumpkin Joe. Ladies and gentlemen, Rebecca Chen, Leigh Ann Jaimes, Sophie St. Pierre, and Margaret Wrobel in . . . *Great Expectations*!"

Rebecca has the easy part. As Biddy, all she has to do is read as she pretends to write her letter to Pip, informing him of Joe's impending arrival. And then she goes offstage to watch the rest of us sweat.

The first part of the scene is really funny. Poor old Joe is not used to wearing nice clothes or being around "gentlemen," and he is really awkward, which makes Pip totally uncomfortable. And Joe never does figure out what to do with his hat; no matter where he sets it, it falls to the floor. He tells the story of a church clerk who has left the church—"had a drop," as he puts it— and joined a group of traveling actors. Pip's roommate, Herbert (played by *moi*), enters and offers him a choice of coffee or tea, and even that decision is unbearably difficult for him. It is only my second-best acting performance of the day, but I manage to maintain my British accent throughout and exit stage right, where I watch the second half with Rebecca.

After Herbert's exit, the scene turns more serious as the negative changes to Pip's nature become more and more apparent. Joe insists on calling Pip "sir," and soon after he explains his reason for the visit—to give Pip a message from Miss Havisham that Estella wishes to see him. Then Joe gets up to leave.

"But you are not going now, Joe?"

"Yes I am," said Joe.

"But you are coming back to dinner, Joe?"

"No I am not," said Joe.

Leigh Ann moves close to Margaret and takes her hand. People in the audience actually set their forks and knives down to listen.

"Pip, dear old chap," Leigh Ann, as Joe, starts, *"life is made of ever so many partings welded together, as I may say . . . Divisions among such must come, and must be met as they come. If there's been any fault at all today, it's mine. You and me is not two figures to be together in London; nor yet anywheres else but what is private, and beknown, and understood among friends. It ain't that I am proud, but that I want to be right, as you shall never see me no more in these clothes . . . You won't find half so much fault in me if you think of me in my forge dress, with my hammer in my hand, or even my pipe . . . And so God bless you, dear old Pip, old*

chap. God bless you!" Leigh Ann touches Margaret's Pip on the forehead and then turns and walks away, joining Rebecca and me in the wings. Margaret is alone onstage, and she looks positively haunted by Leigh Ann's last lines. She turns to the audience to deliver her short final monologue.

"I had not been mistaken in my fancy that there was a simple dignity in him. The fashion of his dress could no more come in its way when he spoke these words than it could come in its way in heaven. He touched me gently on the forehead and went out. As soon as I could recover myself sufficiently, I hurried out after him and looked for him in the neighboring streets; but he was gone."

The auditorium is silent. It is as if people are afraid that breathing might break the spell.

We all run out to join Margaret for our group bow, and the audience—even the eighth graders—explodes into cheers and applause. When it finally dies down, we duck behind the curtain and practically knock over Mr. Eliot, who is about to introduce the next group.

Except for an overwhelmed and underprepared substitute back in the fifth grade, I have never seen a teacher cry, but there is Mr. Eliot, wearing that silly beard, eyes welling.

"Girls, I don't know what to say. I figured you'd be good, but that was beyond all . . . *expectations,* if you will."

Pun intended.

* * *

Another victory for the Red Blazer Girls—we win the award for best skit! Mr. Eliot hands us each a shiny new hardcover copy of *Nicholas Nickleby*. I have just the spot for it in my room.

My mom looks so proud, and I am really stunned when I realize that Dad is still there, too. He had planned to leave after our skit, but when he saw how good we were, he said he had to stay to see us take the prize. He gives me a big hug, and suddenly it's my turn to fight back the tears.

Out of the corner of my eye, I see Margaret hugging her grandmother and then taking her by the hand, introducing her to everyone. When we all converge near the center of the room, Malcolm and Ms. Harriman, *both* in tweed, make their way toward us.

Ms. Harriman hugs us each in turn. "Girls, you were wonderful! I can't remember having a better time, and you absolutely deserved to win. Margaret and Leigh Ann—what can I say? Truly, truly remarkable."

"And this . . ." Malcolm steps aside to reveal the woman standing behind him.

"You must be Caroline," I say. She is so beautiful that I suddenly feel a bit awkward—I am still in men's clothes and makeup.

"You look *just* like you did when you were sixteen," Margaret gushes.

Caroline laughs, her eyes sparkling just like her

father's. "You're very kind. And this is my daughter, Caitlin."

Caitlin, who is wearing the green sweater of our rival school, Faircastle Academy, takes a shy step toward us. "I'm very pleased to meet you," she says with an impressive—and authentic—British accent.

Ms. Harriman is beaming with pride. "Caitlin, meet Sophie St. Pierre, Margaret Wrobel, Rebecca Chen, and Leigh Ann Jaimes. These young ladies have been a tremendous help to me the past couple of weeks. I cannot imagine how they had the time to prepare for this *and* do all that they did."

"We are so happy to finally meet you, Caroline," Margaret says. "We have a little something for you."

"You do?"

Ms. Harriman beams. "A birthday present. From your grandfather."

"From . . . from Grandpa Ev?"

Malcolm tells her about the birthday card and promises to fill in the important details later.

Then Margaret takes the ring off her finger and holds it out to Caroline. "Sorry it doesn't have a nice box or anything, but this is it—the Ring of Rocamadour. Well, one of them."

At first, Caroline seems afraid to touch it. After a few seconds, though, she lifts it from Margaret's hand and holds it up to the light to get a clear look at it. Her hand moves to her mouth, and then to her heart; some feelings she must have kept inside for fifteen years bubble up to the surface.

"I don't know what to say. This is so overwhelming. It's beautiful. And you girls—"

"They did it all," Ms. Harriman says. "They are quite special, the whole bunch of them."

I give Malcolm a playful nudge. "Well, we did have a *little* help."

Malcolm scoffs. "Nonsense. I hardly lifted a finger. You girls deserve all the credit. And on that note, I have a surprise for you. Elizabeth has brought to my attention a certain situation that might cause the breakup of the 'Red Blazer Girls,' as I believe you refer to yourselves. In light of everything that you have done for us, *that* would be totally unacceptable. A travesty, even. So I did some digging around at the university, and I learned that we have an opening for a nurse in our clinic—a position, I believe, that would be very similar to the one your mother is leaving, Miss Chen."

Ms. Harriman cuts in. "We sat next to her during the show and had a very nice talk. She is *very* proud of you, Rebecca."

"I would be happy to put in a good word for her," Malcolm says. "I can't make any promises, but I still have *some* pull at the university."

Rebecca throws her arms around Ms. Harriman and shakes Malcolm's hand. "Thank you, thank you! She is an *awesome* nurse."

"My pleasure. Have your mom give me a call if she has any questions."

"And Rebecca," Ms. Harriman adds, "be sure to tell your mother about the art lessons you're starting next week." More hugging, more screaming, as it all really sinks in: the Red Blazer Girls are here to stay.

Chapter 37

I know I said one more chapter and this makes two, but it's my favorite part, and it's <u>my</u> book, so there

We say our good-byes to Ms. Harriman, and to Malcolm, who has somewhat improbably become like a favorite uncle to us, and to Caroline and Caitlin, who would look *so* much better in a red blazer than in that green Faircastle thing. *Hmmm.* We are about to head backstage to change into our regular clothes when Margaret tugs on my sleeve.

"What?"

"Haven't you forgotten someone?"

"Uh, I don't think so. What are you talking about?"

"Raf."

"Oh my God. Raf! I *completely* forgot. Is he here?" Margaret takes me by the shoulders and spins me so that I face straight back.

He is leaning against a wall, arms crossed. My heart begins to beat a little faster, and I feel my face go red. "God, he must hate me. We totally dissed him."

"We?" says Margaret. "*I* talked to him right after we got the award. You are the only one doing any dissing here."

"You'd better get over there, girl," Rebecca says. "If you don't, I might. He looks really cute tonight."

"Okay, okay!" I don't remember walking across the room, but somehow I find myself in front of him.

"Hey there," I say, wittily and with feeling.

He doesn't say anything, but he does tilt his head back ever so slightly and smile—just a little. The effect is devastating. Does he *know* what he is doing to me?

"I'm sorry, Raf. I just—"

"What are you sorry about?"

"You know. I mean, I ignore your calls and texts all week, and then you come all the way over here to see us, and then I ignore you some more."

He shrugs. "Brought you something." He hands me a bouquet of flowers still wrapped in their paper.

I peek inside. Pink roses—my favorite. "Thanks. I mean, wow, this is so sweet." I go to hug my friend as I've done a million times, but this time it feels . . . different.

And then he does it. Right there in front of God, Margaret, and everybody. He kisses me.

When it starts, I am so surprised that I still have my eyes open! And I swear that the cliché is totally true— my knees actually start to give out. When we finally pull apart, I must have the stupidest look of all time on my face. I still can't say anything. And I can't stop smiling, smiling, smiling. My first real kiss.

"Are you guys okay over there?" Rebecca shouts as she and Margaret and Leigh Ann run toward us, laughing and babbling incoherently.

"It's about time," Margaret says.

That Margaret. She's always right.

Case closed.

Acknowledgments

I am grateful to the many friends, colleagues, family members, and students who have encouraged and inspired me and helped make this book possible. A few individuals deserve extra helpings of appreciation: to Rosemary Stimola for her enthusiasm and willingness to look past the flaws in my first draft, and to Cecile Goyette at Knopf for her faith, insight, and suggestions, and for teaching me a thing or fifty about writing. To Beth Gratzer, Erin Flaherty, Joanne Ptak, Ariella Grinberg, Dorothy Luczak, Fabiane DeSouza, Saoirse McSharry, Denise Coleman, Tammy King, Steve Holub, and Gretchen Bauermeister, all of whom were early readers, sounding boards, and critics. And Lynn Palmer, wherever you are: I'm still trying. But most of all, I thank my wife, Laura Grimmer—best friend, confidante, and enabler-in-chief for fifteen wonderful, amazing years.

Need more mystery?

TEEB AEGR SEUN ONOA OHRH ILNA VNUE
HRDL ZRIL RTRS OFRN TETR LIGD ETR!